Dead on the Rio Grande

Eric Mettenbrink

Chapter 1 – Life as I Knew It.

At times, Mr. Carlisle didn't seem real, like he was a myth or just some sort of aberration stemming from my own mental deficiencies, but he was all too tangible to disclaim. I've concluded that he had great power and intelligence, and a host of people who, whether they knew it or not, assisted him with his deeds.[1] I never really feared him, but thinking about him was uncomfortable and I am obligated to not ignore that he at least existed at one time. I wanted to forget him, but I needed to know how to handle the concept of Mr. Carlisle, because he will always been around, and a person must put on their full armor to face him.[2]

I vividly remember the first time that I met Mr. Carlisle or I vividly recreated the first time I met him, it's hard to say what's real anymore. He first came upon me like lightning falling from the sky[3], yet somehow with a guile subtlety. I was an associate at a large firm with an international presence. You couldn't get much bigger or more important than that firm, our local office location alone had at least two hundred attorneys. If you had this firm on your resume, you were set for almost any position for the rest of your life. Not to mention the fact that it paid well and quite frankly, I liked telling people that I worked there. Eyes would light up followed by nods of approval when I mentioned where I was employed.

I had been there for about a year and a half. I had the lay of the land and felt comfortable about my position. I received a raise after my first year and a bonus. I did good work and for multiple partners. This was my strategy, do good work for many people in case the relationship sours. In other words, if I aligned only with one partner and that partner were to turn on me, nobody would fight to justify my employment because I was just a machine that generated

---

[1] Eph. 6:12
[2] Eph. 6:11, 13
[3] Luke 10:18

billables, which generated the revenue, which paid for all the partners' fun and interesting stuff. That's what it was about. No matter how good a job I would do or how many bills I generated, a partner could still turn on me in a way that was beyond my control. They wanted more stuff and they needed me to bill, so they could get more stuff. That was just how it worked.

A buddy of mine, albeit a temporary buddy, was a good attorney and nobody could deny it. Jeff, I think his name was Jeff, worked for a partner that was in a feud with another partner. The other partner was hanging on to certain associates even though he wasn't generating enough work for them. Jeff's boss pointed this out at a shareholder's meeting, which was not particularly well received by the other partner. As a result, the affronted partner targeted Jeff as his enemy because he couldn't target Jeff's boss. The two partners eventually compromised by trimming some of the associates, including Jeff. Jeff did nothing wrong, but it was a gamble to work for just one boss. A person needs to hedge their bets, even in an employment situation. I hedged my bets all over the place. I was a bet hedger extraordinaire.

The trick was keeping them all happy. It was a shell game. I couldn't tell one boss that I couldn't get to their stuff because I was working on someone else's case, it didn't work like that. No, I needed to tell them that all of their work was the most important and at the top of the list. The problem is that when I juggled all these things, I did a lot of things good, but nothing great, so nobody complained that much, but I wasn't considered a superstar either. It was more about survival, really. I became a master of this boss management technique and felt pretty good about my place in the firm, until I met Mr. Carlisle.

It was the start of the workday and I headed over to the elevators with a group of strangers like I always did, looking straight ahead at the elevator doors and not making any eye contact. Most stared at their phones or had headphones in their ears, so that they could show the

2

world that they weren't interested in conversation. I felt the same way, but I also thought that staring at my phone or listening to music was amateurish. My technique was to look straight ahead at the elevator doors instead, in order to show my fellow passengers that I could have a conversation if I wanted to engage, but will not take the initiative to do so.

Mr. Carlisle stood next to me waiting for the elevator as well. I'd never seen him before, though he seemed familiar to me in certain ways. Maybe the familiarity was based entirely on looks, it was hard to determine. He was slightly below average in height, dressed professionally, bald with reddish-gray hair on the sides of his head, neatly trimmed, clean shaven, non-descript, not intimidating, but not charismatic looking and completely non-threatening in appearance…in appearance that is. His rather plain look is likely why I thought I'd seen him before, because I've seen someone like him a thousand times without knowing it. These plain people, they are part of your peripheral vision, yet they are lodged somewhere in your sub-consciousness permanently. Maybe they're like a certain mug you have on your desk for show. It was a gift or something. You don't notice the mug or pay any attention to it, but if it were moved, your sub-conscious would notice it and you wouldn't feel quite right.

The doors opened to the elevator and Mr. Carlisle turned to me and said, "You go first, I had an elevator case once and I never got over it. They were defective, there was a broken elevator on the left and a working one on the right. This guy wasn't looking when the doors opened to the left one first and he fell all the way down the shaft.[4] If he had just looked or if the elevator on the right had opened first, he wouldn't have splattered thirty stories below. We did a site inspection and the other side was so mad at me, they threatened to throw me down the shaft and seal me up for good."[5] It was a long initial introduction. It was too long and too detailed for

---

[4] Matt. 25:41
[5] Rev. 20:3

a normal person to bring up to strangers. I nodded at him with a slight smile out of discomfort, not from happiness. I of course, looked down at the elevator floor before entering and Mr. Carlisle noticed and chuckled to himself.

"It wasn't this one of course. Ever since that day though, I have someone else go first while I check to see if anyone's behind me, just in case they want to throw me down the shaft," said Mr. Carlisle. I did my fake chuckle, smiled again and promptly looked up at the little television screen in the elevator. Those little screens had become lifesavers for many of us. I stared at it while everyone else stared at their phones. Mr. Carlisle stared at neither.

Mr. Carlisle pushed the button for the forty-fourth floor, which was my floor. This bothered me because I'd never seen him before and he was certainly old enough to be a partner. He had to be a partner or they would have booted him from the firm by then. It was a packed elevator and people were gradually getting off about every other floor or so. Mr. Carlisle seemed to sense that we were headed to the same place.

"What kind of car do you drive?" Mr. Carlisle asked loudly enough for the other passengers to hear. I squirmed and smirked to brush it off. What kind of question was this? Isn't that like asking how much money a person makes? Why was it his business and who cares for that matter? I found his question to be extremely rude, but he was going to the same floor as me and I didn't know who he was, so there was no way I was going to take him to task for it. I tried my fake chuckle again and hoped he would move on.

Mr. Carlisle did not move on. In fact, he continued to wait in silence for my answer. Nobody else was looking at me, just him, but I knew they were listening. Mr. Carlisle was looking directly at me. He did not overt his gaze. Everybody on the elevator looked out of the corner of their eye, that was how people looked at others on elevators, and that was how people looked at each other in the hallways and in the office, unless they needed something from someone. A person doesn't look at someone unless they need something from them…that was the rule. They were listening though. I knew they were listening.

The silence was getting awkward until Mr. Carlisle began again, "It must be a piece of garbage or you would have said something by now…unless it's a super car and you're embarrassed, right? I mean, you're probably thinking that my question was rude, which it could be considered, but not really if you think about it because you don't know my motivation. I could be trying to inform you that it's being towed or that I accidentally ran into it, right? But you think I'm some sort of shallow individual overcompensating and wanting to have a measurement between us. Am I right? What you fail to see is that it doesn't matter. Even if you believe me to be rude and that my question is out of line, if you had a nice car … you would retort and tell me what kind of car you drive. That is a fact. Therefore, all of us in this elevator can conclude that you do not have a nice car." Mr. Carlisle looked around gleefully, as if he were waiting for some kind of applause.

My face grew hot with embarrassment. In theory, I could take out a car loan and buy some entry level high-end foreign car like all the others on my floor, but I was better than that! I had substance! They, through no fault of their own, did not have substance. They just weren't aware of it. It's not prudent to go that far in debt for a car, even if you could easily afford the monthly payments, why keep putting yourself further into debt? For what? A car depreciates as soon as you drive it off the lot, then what? Why should I obsess about a car when it will eventually break down or someone will steal it? I was more concerned about other things, things that can't be stolen or broken.[6] A car is not like real estate, there's no equity in it…so what's the

---

[6] Matt. 6:19-21

point of it? I don't want to marry a woman that only looks at me for my car. I mean, I had a good job, good income, I wasn't a bad person and here this guy shows up and tells me that my car was no good! It was still a good car, it's just older and not particularly unique. The Japanese make a good car and they make them in America! That affordable, sensible car of mine was ranked in the top five for cars that will most likely reach two hundred thousand miles! That's what you look for in a person, a good decision maker, somebody that won't mortgage their future for satellite radio or a screen that tells you your tire pressure is low. I've always known when my tire pressure was low, the tires would be flat!

"Because you don't have a good car, you must not be a successful attorney. Otherwise, you would have a good car. Don't tell me you're being responsible either, because if you are successful enough, you can afford not to be responsible," said Mr. Carlisle glibly. He looked around the elevator again, enjoying his audience who refused to look up at him.

The doors opened on the forty-fourth floor and Mr. Carlisle stepped out. I was stunned by this unprovoked attack and forgot that we were getting off on the same floor. As the doors closed Mr. Carlisle turned back to the elevator and said to the passengers, while focusing his gaze on me, "Don't waste your money on this one, he'd be getting paid more if he was any good. Am I right?" I felt the passengers nodding, although I'm not sure how many of them actually heard the exchange.

With that, the doors closed and I took an unnecessary journey to the fifty-sixth floor with the remaining passengers. Nobody said anything or looked at me, but I knew they were never going to hire me after that very public interaction. I was no use to them and they were no longer any use to me. I rode the elevator back to my floor, fearful that I might see Mr. Carlisle waiting for me to humiliate me some more. This time in front of my co-workers. What if he was a client? That was an even more horrifying thought than if he were a partner. What if he was a client...what if he was a client? He would see me, turn to the partner and have me fired with a snap of the fingers.

The doors opened and I didn't see Mr. Carlisle anywhere. I skulked back to my office, shut the door and began to work. It was a big firm, he could be anywhere, but I doubt he knew my name. Once I shut the door, I felt fairly safe. I tried not to let Mr. Carlisle's bullying impact me, for in spite of his behavior, I was sure of what I hoped for with my career and certain of it, even if I couldn't fully see it at the moment.[7]

Eventually, as mortifying of an incident as that elevator encounter was, it faded from my forethought. I didn't see Mr. Carlisle for the rest of the day. In fact, it would be three years before I actually bumped into him again and it was a wonderful three years from what I can recall.

I married shortly after the elevator incident, which I'm sure contributed to me internalizing the insult so severely...due to the pressure of the wedding. I say this not to put a damper on the wedding itself, but it is a fact that getting married is a stressful time. I was told that the ceremony, the dress, the colors, the venue, the guest list, the linens, the honeymoon, the catering, where to have the ceremony, where to have the reception, the cake, the rehearsal dinner, whether to throw rice (nobody threw rice at that time), whether to leave the reception in a limo or a town car because limos seem a bit overdone, and so forth were all extremely stressful.

Then it was the honeymoon. Traveling is a bit much in that when going somewhere beachy, things don't seem to be organized. You really need to get to the airport at least a couple hours in advance. The airline we took was not going to let you get on the plane once boarding

---

[7] Misinterpretation of Heb 11:1

was complete. In other words, you need to get to the plane twenty minutes before takeoff because if you show up twenty-one minutes before takeoff, they don't let you get on the plane to your assigned seat, which remains empty for the rest of the flight because you got there in twenty-one minutes instead of twenty minutes before takeoff! That alone requires thirty minutes extra, giving yourself ten minutes of a buffer to use the restroom or account for mistakes or other delays. While many people don't like a flight at six-thirty in the morning, I preferred it because you just take travel time into account of your commute to the airport and do not need to worry about excessive traffic. That means I really just needed to leave the house forty-five minutes before I needed to get to the airport, but really an hour and half because my wife tended to take at least forty-five minutes longer than I would in order to get ready in the morning. So, we would either get to the airport really early or just on time, which were both acceptable results.

The night before you travel, you should go over your travel list carefully. Packing is easy, but you want to make sure the paper is not delivered as it will tip off any criminals that you are not at home. I still got the paper at that time because I liked to tangibly look at the box scores and compare them as opposed to scrolling through on my phone. You also have to make sure that nobody mentions to the world on social media that you are leaving for vacation and if they do, they should take it down. My wife has lots of friends on social media that publicly praise her and so forth about her going on a vacation. They often specify where we are going and for how long, which is unacceptable.

My wife also needed to make sure the dog was boarded, I just got a dog at the time and it seemed great. A criminal could easily dispatch with a dog, but it is an unwanted nuisance for them and they would most likely move on to a neighbor's house if given a choice. In other words, the dog helped prevented break-ins because it barked at the door as soon as he or she heard the slightest noise. I appreciated that aspect of the dog. I didn't have a window on my front door, which was an advantage because nobody could see the size of the dog and as far as the potential intruder was concerned, the dog may or may not be really big. It had a deceitful bark. Ideally, we would have had two dogs that may or may not be really large. I was told that if you get a little dog that was excitable and put it with a larger dog, the little dog would cause the larger dog to bark more. Unfortunately, I didn't want to add more cleaning, food and backyard scooping to my daily duties. So, we stuck with one dog.

All the bills needed to be paid, the dishes needed to be in the dishwasher, and any plants needed be watered as well. If I had to leave my garbage at the curb, I would have a neighbor or loved one bring it in once the garbage is picked up so the criminals would not know that the house was vacant. We parked our cars inside the garage and shut the doors every day, so nobody from the street could determine if we were home unless they watched us leave. Most of my neighbors that parked their cars outside of the garage have probably been robbed I assumed.

I liked clear plastic bags for my toiletries because I never knew when the security line rules would change and I didn't want someone rifling through my stuff to figure out if my toothpaste was a bomb or not. I wore slip on shoes as a time saver, I never brought my computer for a pleasure trip, always wore long pants and a short sleeved button-up shirt. Shorts and t-shirts don't have a place at the airport because passengers don't want to see a man's legs and one should dress decently when out and about anyway. A suit for a pleasure trip would be excessive and went out in the sixties, which was fine. It's just an airplane. I never understood formalities with travel. On the other hand, there was nothing more offensive to me than seeing a woman wearing sweatpants and carrying a pillow around the airport like it was a sleepover or having some guy wearing a sleeveless shirt putting luggage over my head and displaying his underarms for everyone to see, or his yellowing toes because he decided he wanted to wear flip-flops to the airport. I'd seen flip-flops one too many times at the airport. They would walk through security barefoot! I couldn't fathom the massive amount of diseases stuck to the bottom of their bare feet!

Once at the gate, I could relax and wait for boarding. It was always better to get in line early because even though we had assigned seats, some people still could get confused and I always preferred to get to my seat first in order to avoid conflict.

The honeymoon, once we arrived, was a pretty good time. I felt like my wife and I got closer, although we had some tiffs about my sunburn. I got severely sunburned, which limited some of my activities for the rest of the week or at least made them less enjoyable, which showed outwardly and made her time less enjoyable as well.

Shortly thereafter, we added a baby boy to the family. My wife took some time off work when our son was born, then got right back to it once we found an appropriate nanny. I can't remember how many weeks she got off work for maternity leave, but it didn't seem very long. It wasn't long before we or she was pregnant again. At the time, I believe we were supposed to say "we" were pregnant, as opposed to "she" being pregnant, which was fine. This time we had a girl, so the hand-me-downs weren't really an option and the kids were too close in age to pass down the crib. So, we needed to get a certain amount of new stuff for this one as well. It was expensive, but we had two incomes.

I didn't like the idea of taking out a loan for a car or leasing one, so I was stuck with the same car I'd had for years. No upgrades yet, not that I'd needed or desired one, it was just not an option in the first place, so a discussion about it wouldn't be warranted. It really wouldn't have been my car anyway because my wife and I shared everything, so technically I could drive the

SUV and she could drive my sedan if appropriate. It just so happened that I never wanted to drive the SUV and my wife never wanted to drive my sedan, so it worked out fine.

The nanny seemed okay, but at some point we were going to transition the boy to a preschool to get him acclimated and socialized with other children. He might develop lifelong contacts, so it was important to get him enrolled. We also wanted to teach him boundaries and how to properly behave in a controlled setting. I had a cousin who was a bit older than me. She had two teenagers and I heard story after story of them getting into trouble. We decided that that was not going to be an issue with our son. We wanted to set boundaries and mold his behavior early.

Work was going well at the time, I was handling some larger cases and really getting involved with the partners. The clients loved me. They loved that I was responsive. Even if I couldn't get them an answer or give them a good response, I would let them know I couldn't respond. Clients wanted to know that they were not being ignored. Constant responses. They didn't want to pay massive legal fees to be ignored. I probably spent sixty percent of my work day responding to email questions from clients. Nothing will kill a career quicker than a partner getting a complaint from a client specifically about a lack of responsiveness. Partners liked responses as well, so did my wife and my kids.

Because of my good work, my billable hours and my friendly disposition, I was appointed to my firm's pro bono committee. While I wasn't the final decision maker on the pro bono cases we handled, I did get to personally handle a large portion on my own, which gave me invaluable legal experience that otherwise wouldn't be available to me.

This also went along nicely with my new found enthusiasm with our local church. We had been members for some time, but I'd decided to kick it up a notch and become further involved and I thought it changed me for the better. I started attending more church activities, volunteering my time and reading more religious books when I had the opportunity. I also wanted to lay down a moral foundation for the kids.

My own habits and tendencies had begun to change as well. I rarely drank alcohol, not so much for abstinence sake, but for a broader moral aspect and to test my self-discipline. This became an issue once because my great aunt was a proponent of teetotalism and she let everyone know how wrong it was to drink and how you must be a rotten person if you partook. I remember a time when she was starting her finger wagging again at a family reunion. I got publicly drunk out of spite. It was a bad scene and my wife did not speak to me for roughly a week. That was not a social drinking occasion, but an occasion to prove a point. It was a poor way to prove a point as it turns out because I just embarrassed myself, and my wife. I had also thoroughly confused my boy because of how disproportionately fun I'd become. Worse, my actions proved my great aunt's point. I since fully admitted that my behavior was terrible and abstained for the most part, not for moral purposes, but for practical purposes.

I also began to watch how I spoke around others, fewer swear words and less locker room humor. Most of all, my temper had faded a bit. While in the past, my family's less desirable qualities would have driven me crazy, but after my new commitment to church and family life, I found our differences endearing.

Everything was going quite well with very few bumps or curves in the road. Then, Mr. Carlisle came back into my life and things changed, because I was naive of his designs.[8]

---

[8] Reference to 2 Co. 2:11

Chapter 2. The Incident at the Border

I came in to work, looked at the news for about five minutes, got my coffee, four bottles of water and checked my calendar in order to determine which project was most urgent. Usually, order of importance was determined by which boss was causing the most problems with me. I chose something that was urgent, yet mundane to start my day.

Within an hour or so, I got a message that a partner wanted to see me in one of the conference rooms. I could only imagine that this was either going to be a very bad meeting or very good one. You didn't meet in a conference room with a partner if it wasn't really bad or really good. I had done nothing wrong, nor has my work been nothing but above board. However, things happen. One time, a particularly important client did not approve of how a case was proceeding. It was not the firm's fault as this particular judge was slow and things tended to be prolonged in his courtroom. Unfortunately, the longer a case prolongs, the more money is lost by the client in attorney fees and whatever else is being held up by the lack of resolution of that particular case. As it turned out, a slow courtroom is not an acceptable excuse for a client bleeding money by the hour. So, the partner fired the associates working on the case. The partner knew that the associates weren't responsible. However, numbers were crunched, this was a high paying client, which brought more value to the firm than these particular associates who could be replaced by any of the cold resumes piled on the desk of human resources. I've seen enough of these situations to understand that a person can do everything exactly right, and still be fired…not laid off, but fired.

So, what good could come of this meeting? Not much, if one were to run through the scenarios. Most likely it was to find out if I could work on another project, which I didn't mind. However, there was always some sort of politics behind the scenes. Maybe this partner wanted to use up my time and poach me off of another, not out of necessity, but as measuring stick. A lot of us were used as pawns in these sort of games. I didn't mind, as I always felt comfortable navigating such waters. It certainly wasn't a raise, as that would show up around the holidays on my pay check, not by a meeting or an announcement.

I knocked on the conference room door and carefully made my way in, the partner looked up as if startled that I actually appeared. He had some papers shuffled about, smiled at me and gestured for me to sit. He mentioned that human resources felt as if I would be good at helping out with the pro bono department of the firm. They like to have a partner in charge and an associate helping out to one day take over. Basically, I would be running the show and the partner was there by name only, which would allow him to get the credit, not lose any billable time and blame me if things went wrong. Because of that dynamic, I initially viewed such a position as a negative. I felt like the firm really only did free legal work as an image booster and not out of concern for those that couldn't afford legal representation. There was very little upside to such responsibility. Besides being blamed if things went wrong, nobody gives you points at the firm for charitable endeavors. They said that a certain amount of billable hours were allotted to you for pro bono work, but everyone knew better. At the end of the year, if there was a dent in your hours because of charity work, you were going to be penalized. There was no cash flow from charity and you are therefore less profitable.

However, in recent months I had begun to undergo a shift in how I valued success. If I based my worldview on social media, television, movies and just listening to co-workers, then success would be defined by earnings and how many hours a person dedicates to their job. This would be an unquenchable thirst.

First of all, if hard work and long hours were all it took to be financially successful, then the guy that mowed my lawn would be a billionaire. Hard work is a necessary ingredient, but it's a myth perpetuated in this country that we can all be rich if we just work really hard. We can't all be rich, and if we were, then by definition, nobody would be rich. Intelligence, education, family background, health, luck, opportunities, timing, background, questionable ethics and connections all played a role. The most effective and efficient way to become rich is to be born rich. Be born rich and you have obtained success. Additionally, a person has a much greater chance to become wealthy if that person knows a wealthy person rather than working hard. But one still must try to be successful, because otherwise that person is not productive. If success is defined by money, then a person must be completely motivated by money in order to be successful. Unfortunately, a person who loves money will not be satisfied with money, nor a person who loves wealth with their income, it's all vanity and never ending.[9] At least that's what I thought.

My own personal growth and religious enlightenment led me to redefine success and productivity. Without a doubt, I decided that I must be productive at work. As much as I would have liked an excuse not to try hard at work, I had to work hard because these partners are the people who allowed me to take care of my family, to eat, to have shelter, clothes, entertainment and to live.[10] I owed a duty to my firm.[11] I often wondered what I would say to someone if I were asked about my life. What if God were doing the asking? Most likely, I would be asked what I did to give back to society, help others and share my beliefs. Mentioning a type of car, the size of my house or how lovely my children and spouse were would be laughable to someone

---

[9] Eccl. 5:10
[10] Prov. 12:24
[11] Col. 3:22; Rom. 12:11; 2 Tim. 2:15

who created the entire universe. Nobody in the afterlife would care about my handicap on the golf course, the pictures my wife posted about the food she ate or the exoticness of our vacation.[12] This meeting about our pro bono program was going to be the first step in changing my definition of success. I could not conform any longer to the pattern of the world, but I would be transformed by the renewing of my mind.[13] The motivation of the firm and the negative consequences were irrelevant to the good works in the end and I could let everyone know it.

After a brief conversation, the partner wanted me working on a case near the border. It was an immigration issue. It was a nasty one and would throw my life into a chaos I could never imagine. This was a "hot button", which the firm loved because it was going to give them media attention and in theory bring in more clients.

I had been to one of the cities down there once before for a hearing. That was the closest I'd come to the border for work. It was a small matter and a routine hearing about an insurance claim or something. I couldn't remember. The federal judge down there handled both civil and criminal cases, so while I was waiting for my case to be called, I had to sit through a criminal hearing. Unbeknownst to me, I had sat down right behind the criminal. I don't say "alleged" criminal because this was just the sentencing phase of the matter. The jury had found him guilty a while back and this was just the Judge's turn to make sure the punishment fit the crime. There was an athletic woman sitting to my right and just behind the criminal. She was sitting upright with legs tapping in an excited and alert position. She was dressed formally with a sport coat. On the other side of the courtroom was a man sitting exactly the same way, also wearing a sport coat, each of them darting their eyes about the room. I saw a badge on them and later found out that they were U.S. Marshals. The defense attorney began to call witnesses, mostly family

---

[12] Eccl. 9:10
[13] Rom. 12:2

members to the stand to testify what a great guy the criminal was and how this was a one time deal. With each witness, the marshals would get up and switch locations with each other and a new one showed up behind me and remained standing.

I finally noticed the chains around the prisoner's ankles and realized that I was directly in the line of fire if something went wrong. What a stupid predicament. One should never sit close to the guy in chains while in a courtroom. Of course, it was a silly fear. If anybody was going to kill this guy, it would probably be while he was in prison. He was a Mexican truck driver. He claimed he had never done this before, but who really knows? I believed him for some reason. He had several benign looking family members testify of how long he worked for this particular trucking company and how he was a good dad, husband and son. In a way, they were all telling him goodbye.

The DEA agent that testified said that he asked the criminal repeatedly why he didn't think it was strange that his load was basically empty on this particular delivery. Usually he carried a full load of products to be taken across the border. The agent testified that he asked the criminal how then could he make money on a trucking job that took him from the center of Mexico all the way into the United States with a load that weighed barely a third of his normal load?

This type of thing happened a lot. A poor Mexican truck driver was tempted by the cartel to haul a load of meth to the states with more money and less effort than what was required of his usual job. In the overall scheme of things, the truck driver was taking the biggest risk and was paid a pittance compared to the other players involved. In this instance, the Judge believed that the guy wasn't part of the grand scheme of things. He was a truck driver who was convinced to take the job. He may or may not have done something like this in the past, but it didn't really

17

matter. All it took was one time. Most of the punishment was mandatory. I listened as the Judge explained to this guy's daughter that her father was going away to prison and when he gets out, he will be deported. He also told her that all it takes is one mistake, one time giving into to these cartel guys and your life was ruined forever. It was all true, of course, but I was sure that it stung nonetheless. The Judge rolled back the sentence due to his belief that this guy was just a randomly hired transporter, who had no prior record. The guy got one hundred and fifty months. He was hauled away through the side door. He did not look at his family.

That's what we all were in life, to a certain extent, bit players…people that take the fall and do the work for others who are smarter, more charismatic or lack a sufficient conscious to stop short of crossing the line dividing good and evil or more accurately the line between consideration and disregard of other's lives. To the sociopath go the spoils.

A few days after my meeting with the partner, I was on a plane to the Rio Grande Valley. The full details weren't known to me at the time, but it was an issue and the firm would get a massive amount of press for helping out in this situation. It was all about illegal immigration. No matter what side the firm was on, half the country would support it and the other half would not, but all would look at the firm and know about it.

The kid's name was Jairo Ortiz. He was as the local authorities say, "OTM" or "other than Mexican". I say kid, because he was a minor. His exact age is probably unknown because I'm guessing Honduras doesn't keep the greatest birth certificate records in the world. Generally speaking in the modern era, countries where people are risking their lives to flee from their home due to excessive violence are countries that lack organizational structure and tight records. Chaos breeds chaos and Honduras at the time was chaotic. There was no peace for a person who left Honduras or to anyone who came in, as there were many disturbances afflicting the inhabitants of that land.[14] I didn't know why Honduras was the most recent South or Central American country that had devolved into violence, but it was. Costa Rica was fine and was right next door. Why were two neighbors so different?

About Jairo Ortiz, we had a minor from Honduras who illegally crossed the border into Texas. Now what? Did we need to send him back or keep him here? This was a growing problem with the states at the border because more and more unaccompanied minors were showing up and needed to be fed and sheltered before determining the next step. This next step was the point of contention with a lot of people, including many of my acquaintances. Feeding and sheltering the minors was easy. Most of us didn't disagree that we should take care of these kids for at least a certain amount of time. The question is whether to deport them or allow them to stay with a pathway to citizenship. If you want to deport them, where do you send them? Do you stick them on a flight back to Honduras and wish them good luck? Is it our duty to find their families and reunite them? Is it cheaper just to let them stay? If you do let them stay, who takes care of them? If you allow private citizens to take care of these kids, how do you vet them? A person could run through an infinite amount of different scenarios and no overwhelmingly satisfactory solution could be made.

All that being said, the story of Jairo Ortiz was even more complicated. I didn't know how much was true as I received all my information third-person, so it was hard to say where assumptions became truth in these accounts. Also, much of the information gathered was from other travelers or witnesses that were likely partaking in less than legal activities.

However, a lot of information came from one of the shelters on the other side of the river at Reynosa. It was church sponsored and provided food and shelter for those that failed to cross

---

[14] 2 Chr. 15:5

the border, were ripped off by coyotes or who were deported and didn't have the funds to go home or try again. Apparently, Jairo had run out of funds before crossing the border. One of the men from the shelter came upon Jairo, and when he saw him, he felt compassion. [15] My understanding was that Jairo wasn't particularly talkative, but one of the men running the shelter was able to coax some background information out of him, at least about his journey. The village where Jairo was born and raised in Honduras had become a desperate situation for his family. People were dying on the streets, it was rarely safe to even scratch out the most meager of a living for the family to survive. Somebody had to take a chance to get to the United States because the reward far outweighed the risk. Whatever one could earn just doing manual migrant work was far greater than what a person could earn in the village. Most importantly, it was just a matter of time before one would die. Jairo was the oldest child and would make the journey. His father stayed behind to look after the family. Once Jairo began earning money, the plan was that he would send it home and each member would come over a bit at a time. Even the most desperate situation in the States was better than Jairo's village.

Jairo's family gave him whatever money they had and they made arrangements for his passage. An upfront fee was paid and Jairo had some extra money for the rest of the way. Unfortunately, by the time Jairo had reached Reynosa, he was out of funds. Most of his money was taken from him at Tecum Uman in Guatemala, and the rest was taken at Arriaga.

The robbery in Tecum Uman was a trick and Jairo blamed himself in his naivety. A man had approached him, claiming that he was supposed to lead Jairo to the next part of his journey for the next portion of his fee. Usually, everyone along the way of these journeys took a little extra than what was promised and initially paid. In this instance, this man was just a local taking

---

[15] Luke 10:33

money from Jairo. In other words, the local man saw an opportunity to rip off a traveler and was successful.

Arriaga was a different story. Jairo wasn't tricked, he was just robbed. A couple of boys approached him, pulled out knives and took his money and that was the end of it. There was nothing he could have done to avoid it other than having a little better luck.

I saw a nature show once about a sloth swimming across a river in a South American jungle. There it was, slowly struggling across the river, stroke by stroke. The river was full of crocodiles, yet the sloth for some reason needed to get to the other side. The sloth had no way of protecting itself against the crocodiles or caimans or whatever they were calling them on the show, and yet, the sloth still tried to swim across even though there was nothing it could do to stop from being killed if a crocodile was so inclined to eat it. Somehow this sloth had made it across the river. It did nothing at all to prevent itself from being eaten, for if a crocodile wanted to eat it, the crocodile would do so. It just so happened that at that moment in time, the crocodiles either didn't see the sloth or just didn't feel like eating the sloth. In the same way, anyone could have been robbed at Arriaga at any time, it's whether the victim happened to have been noticed by the robber. Sometimes a man will just fall among robbers until he is stripped, beaten and left half dead.[16] All you can do is hope someone out there will have some compassion for you.

According to the men that ran the shelter, Jairo was out of money after Arriaga. He had managed to make it as far as Reynosa, but that is where the journey stopped. Unfortunately for Jairo, he had heard of a different way to cross the river without the need for immediate funds.

---

[16] Luke 10:30

The men at the shelter warned of this type of arrangement, but Jairo was set on crossing no matter the downside.

For those without money, there were coyotes around that would make arrangements for border crossings and then the illegal immigrant would arrange to pay back the debt later. This is a silly notion for anyone with sense would know that it would never be this simple otherwise everyone would make such an arrangement. In theory, you promise to pay someone back the cost of crossing the border and you could just disappear once on the other side. This would seem like a no-brainer. Unfortunately, most of those involved in trafficking, whether it be trafficking of people or drugs, are tied in some degree to a drug cartel or organization. So whether you know it or not, if you make such an arrangement with these kind folks, they will make sure the debt is paid back three times. You could be crossing with drugs, picking up drugs on the other side, or in some cases once a person crosses the border, they are immediately in possession of someone from that drug organization on the other side of the river and they will find all sorts of horrible ways for you to pay the debt. As with any criminal lender, the debt will never be fully paid.

Jairo made such an arrangement. Then things got really complicated. For a long time, the Zetas controlled Reynosa, but at that time of Jairo's crossing, it seemed as if control was up for grabs. When control is up for grabs, lots of bad things happen or a greater number of bad things happen than usual. When an up and coming organization wants to make a mark and control a territory, they conduct business in an extreme and bold manner. When an incumbent organization wants to maintain power and hold off an up and coming organization, they conduct business in and extreme and bold manner. I don't know exactly what happened between Jairo making the arrangements with the new coyote and the events that followed, all I know about is the aftermath, which was horrendous.

The coyote was part of a larger group of traffickers, which decided to handle the human trafficking as well as drug trafficking, no more middle man as the stakes had become higher. The cartels didn't like to bother with human trafficking as the risk weight reward wasn't there. Far more money could be made transporting drugs in the same space that could be used to transport humans. Drugs don't die, drugs are far more valuable and drugs don't become witnesses. Human trafficking was left to lower tier criminals. Far more work was required to get humans across the border for a tiny amount of money. Big organizations traditionally didn't want to bother with it.

The timing of the border crossing was particularly interesting as it was right before sunset. Nobody crossed when it was light outside. It was just common sense. They crossed when it was dark. Jairo with nine others were crammed into an inflatable raft and attempted to cross the border, before the sun went down, right across where a Texas game warden was making her final rounds of the day. The fact that I use the pronoun "her" should not be overlooked. There are very few women game wardens in Texas, so it was no insignificant feat that she was there. Of course the Game Warden saw the raft as it was over stuffed, which resulted in some unavoidable commotion. After the raft got more than halfway to the other side of the river, the Game Warden began to make a call to dispatch for the border patrol or local law enforcement to come by and pick the group up once they landed. Before the Game Warden could finish the call, her voice was drowned out by blood curdling screams as the raft suddenly burst into flames. The raft instantly became an inferno and the ten people trying to cross the border were starting to burn to death. It was a river of fire.[17] According to the Game Warden, it

23

was a mass scramble to get into the water, arms flailing in panic and pain, screams of terror and chaos.

The Game Warden changed the call to first responders and jumped into the water to bring these charred souls to shore. All ten made it to Texas in various degrees of agony, some under their own power, others came ashore with help from the Warden and still others were dragged in face down. The reports indicated that three died on the scene. The Game Warden, border patrol, city police and the sheriff's department were all on the scene along with fire and EMS. By all accounts, it was a terrible tragedy. While many of these unfortunate victims made the decision to cross the border out of desperation, it was nonetheless a bad decision and they were rebuked. They were rebuked and judgment was executed with flames of fire.[18]

Jairo Ortiz was apparently the only minor of the group and he was severely burned to the point of unrecognition. Jairo was our pro bono case. I didn't know much about immigration law, public interest law or anything involving juvenile law, but I was on the case. I'd assume that I would get instructions on how to proceed once I arrived in South Texas, which was going to serve as my home base for this matter.

My plane landed and I began to think about how complicated this was going to be and how in the dark I was about everything. Little did I know that things were actually going to become much more complicated. I eventually made it to my hotel.

As I walked through the hotel doors, I noticed him sitting in the lobby reading a newspaper. Short, bald with glasses, still well dressed and unassuming. If I never met him before I would think he was just someone's goofy uncle or father. Mr. Carlisle looked up from the paper as soon as I entered the lobby and smiled at me as our eyes met. I was astonished to

---

[17] Rev. 20:15
[18] Isa. 66:15-16

24

see him. Out of all the places and chance encounters, how could this guy who I briefly met on an elevator ride once, be sitting in front of me in the exact same hotel as me, in the Rio Grande Valley of Texas? My mouth hung open for a bit as I immediately became nervous. The firm must have sent him, but why?

He seemed genuinely glad to see me as he greeted me and gleefully said, "There's a change in plans."

Chapter 3 – Steak Dinner.

Mr. Carlisle and I met for dinner that night. I was ready to get to work and suggested that we eat at the hotel restaurant, but he refused. He insisted that we eat at a steak house he favored and he even offered to pay as a way of sealing the deal.

It was a dark place, seemingly from the past and it even had a piano player in the background. The darkness permeated the place, like a cave, but with twinkling of dinner candles evenly distributed. It was a bit of a struggle for the candles, but ultimately the light shines in the darkness, and the darkness cannot overcome it.[19] Mr. Carlisle was already seated with a scotch, watching the pianist with a smile. His mind seemed to be drifting off to some distant memory of sorts, some place that seemed a bit wistful to him. I didn't care to ask. He appeared pleasant enough in this state of mind without me interrupting. I asked for a water and buried my face in the menu until Mr. Carlisle finally spoke.

"I've been hearing a lot of great things about you," he said with a smile. The statement floored me given that the last time Mr. Carlisle and I interacted seemed to be him just being a bully to a random person. Strangely, the compliment was much more flattering coming from him than someone else. That's the great tragedy of flattery. You can receive compliments left and right from loved ones, people that actually care about you, but nothing compares to a compliment from a person you were at odds with at some point in time. Flattery from an abuser tastes much more sweet and will more likely than not wash away any sort of ill will that previously existed. It's a mind game that's self-perpetuated, but nonetheless fully effective. He knew nothing of me, yet Mr. Carlisle had put me at ease with just one phrase, a phrase so vague that it should be devoid of all value, but it wasn't. What great things? What was I possibly

---

[19] John 1:5

doing at the firm that was considered great? Actually, he didn't even specify that these "great things" were regarding my work. What did I do that was great outside of work? I was a good dad and husband, but he wouldn't know about that…was I great? No greater than anyone else. Every now and then I did some volunteer work, but was it great? No greater than anyone else collecting an offering plate. I wasn't a part of any leadership committee, I hadn't changed anybody for the better. I wasn't a mentor. I knew of people my age that actually created their own charities or were on the board of a charity. I was never asked to be on a board of anything, nor did I have the time to create a charity of any kind. Nothing I've done in my entire life could be interpreted as great.

Then the thought occurred that I might be undervaluing my achievements. In comparison to the rest of the world, I might be great. Maybe the other associates weren't that good, maybe the bar had been lowered. A lot of the others at the firm were terrible parents and spouses. They never saw their kids, they cheated on their spouses…they played golf all day on the weekends. I was devoted to work, family, even God…even God during a time when you weren't supposed to be devoted to a god or the God. You could get into some real trouble espousing such things, especially at work. We were back to carving fish into the bottoms of doors. We also couldn't criticize those here were religious either. We couldn't espouse it or criticize it, almost as if the goal was to just not acknowledge such things all together. We were frightened of things beyond our control.

I had two sets of neighbors who had kids, one had teenagers the other had little ones. If you have little children, you make plans, take actions, set parameters, control information intake, determine the best way to educate, eat, love, etc., in order to mold these children into your vision of what they should be when they become adults. If a child grows up to be less than the ideal mold of an adult, it can easily be attributed to the parents' lack of effort, knowledge or will to raise such a child. If that parent would have just done certain things differently, then that child would have been fine...like mine. Making sure that our children grow up to be "fine" would be an insult actually, not a goal, the goal is success as defined by the parent. Nobody wants to give into the fact that there are certain physical, mental and outside influences that may mold a child a certain way beyond a parent's best efforts. A parent cannot will a genetic disease to disappear from a child, it was likely there before the child was born and well beyond any influence of the parent. The whole prospect of having a lack of control is uncomfortable and acknowledgment of an all knowing and omnipresent being that created the entire world in which we live is the epitome of lack of control and self determined destiny.

So I was out there, on my own, possibly doing something great or setting an example for those to follow. Why couldn't "good things" be heard about me too? I assumed Mr. Carlisle must have been a big deal if people were approaching him and telling him "good things" about me.

There we were, Mr. Carlisle ordered a steak and another scotch. I ordered a steak as well, a cheaper cut, but a steak nonetheless. I didn't want something too expensive because it might be perceived as arrogance. The steak was delicious.

As we began to eat, Mr. Carlisle snapped my newly found comfort with some unfortunate news, "You're border kid didn't make it." The matter of fact nature in Mr. Carlisle's delivery jolted me. I never even got the chance to interview the kid, Jairo. I stared, dumbfounded at Mr. Carlisle for a moment, waiting for him to admit it was a joke. He could perceive my disbelief and continued, "The burns were massive. It's my understanding that the raft was soaked with some sort of fuel that went up real quick." This was all that Mr. Carlisle decided to disclose, he didn't see any necessity to proceed with further details.

I found out later that the raft was drenched in diesel or something and once the raft got further out in the river and closer to the American side, someone from the bank threw a Molotov cocktail onto the raft to ignite it. The whole thing was bizarre. I couldn't figure out what was to gain by such a senseless act. Most of the stories I read about the cartels would lead me to believe that they wouldn't bother with something like this. Why would they retaliate or set an example with some poor migrants, who probably half of which weren't even Mexican? Nothing made sense and Mr. Carlisle didn't care enough to examine the issue any further.

"You've got a new task. I need you to meet with a judge at some point this week while you're down here," Mr. Carlisle said.

"Are we representing the others?" I asked. Mr. Carlisle nodded.

My understanding was that we were likely going to represent some of the survivors of the incident, especially if there were any additional minors involved. Most of these people were severely burned and would require an extensive stay at the burn facility before anyone could even determine what to do with them. The whole thing was a mess and I assumed we were involved in order to sort things out and to make sure the migrants understood what was happening and that they could make an informed decision about their future. In the meantime, Mr. Carlisle told me that I was supposed to bring over some briefing for the state criminal Judge that was handling some charges against the bad guys. Someone on our side of the river might have participated in the nasty affair and might have some charges against them. We weren't exactly sure how the jurisdictional issues were going to play out, but we wanted the Judge and

Prosecutor to have our briefing regarding the extensive injuries to the victims, so that they would know the full extent of the harm that took place as a result of these horrible deeds.

"So am I going down to interview the victims?" I asked Mr. Carlisle.

"Nope, we've already done the legwork on that. You are just going to deliver the documents to the Judge and the Prosecutor. We've got at least one person dead, so that will have an effect on the charges as well as the severity of the rest. The court system down here is overwhelmed and we are just helping move things along. The Prosecutor and Judge need the full story from us as well as law enforcement. You'll have a briefcase at the front desk probably in the morning. It's locked and not meant to be opened by anyone other than the Judge or Prosecutor. This is a matter of safety for the victims," explained Mr. Carlisle.

I was puzzled. I wasn't a criminal lawyer, so I wasn't familiar with the process, but it seemed strange to give the Judge and Prosecutor information ahead of time like this. It also didn't seem ethical to communicate with the Judge in that way either. On the other hand, if the Prosecutor knew about it, then what's the harm? If some of these victims are minors, then I certainly understood why we would keep the identities confidential, but locking them in a briefcase seemed extreme. Most importantly, why was I not a part of the initial investigation?

Mr. Carlisle seemed to sense my questions and began to answer, "You are too important for the grunt work of interviewing these victims. This could be dangerous and local people would be a better fit. These people aren't going to open up to someone like you, right? They needed to talk to a local, bilingual person if you get what I'm saying." I nodded and he continued, "Besides, you're the guy that needs to be communicating with the Judge and Prosecutor, you're the face of the firm that needs to be out front with the judiciary and media. Let everyone else take care of the groundwork."

I was once again flattered by Mr. Carlisle's confidence in me. I assumed he was probably right. I needed to be focused on the big stuff not the details. I would take the briefing to the Judge the next day and wait for further instruction.

Mr. Carlisle soon turned to small talk and left the legal matters behind for the rest of the evening. Most of the talk was the typical questions about my flight, how's my family and so on. Every time that I tried to ask Mr. Carlisle about his family, he would divert the conversation back to me and my life. He was even reluctant to share with me mundane details, such as travel topics. I had asked him if he was coming from back home or in between stops and he just said that he'd been "going to and fro".[20] Then once again he would turn the conversation to me. It was strange, yet probably the most anybody has ever seemed interested in me, which includes most of my friends and family. Then he became a bit philosophical.

Mr. Carlisle quipped, "A man can't walk on hot coals and not scorch his feet, right?"[21] I had no idea what exactly he was referencing. Mr. Carlisle sensed my confusion and continued, "I mean, these people, they want to cross the border. It's a dangerous trek, so such things are part of the process, right? That's what I mean, you can't walk on hot coals and not scorch your feet. They got scorched all right, wouldn't you say?" I nodded, but was uncomfortable with how lightly he was taking the matter. A minor died after taking on a tremendous journey. He didn't die peacefully either. I couldn't imagine many worse ways to die than succumbing to burns.

I helped out on a case when I was a clerk that is still in the back of my mind to this day. It was a pipeline explosion. There was a hole in the pipeline that needed to be welded shut. The foreman decided that he would weld it on the spot. There was some miscommunication and he

---

[20] Job 1:7
[21] Prov. 6:28

thought the valve was closed, but it wasn't. He was blown a hundred yards away and suffered burns from his scalp all the way down to the soles of his feet. He lasted about four days before he died. Medical bills and documents needed to be provided to the defendant in the wrongful death case, so I had to review them for privileged information before sending them out. It included pictures of the meshed skin grafts the doctors performed. The guy looked like a pile of old meat being pressed up against some chicken wire. Luckily, he was mostly unconscious through the ordeal. I read testimony from his wife discussing the fact that she had no idea that was her husband lying there in the hospital. I mean, she knew it was him because somebody told her, but he had no physical resemblance to her husband. That experience alone made Mr. Carlisle's comment distasteful to me and I decided to mention as much.

"I'm not sure if it's the same thing. I mean…getting robbed, being hungry or thirsty, even drowning might be something they expected, but being lit on fire doesn't sound like anything a person would expect if crossing the border," I retorted, still trying to maintain a friendly demeanor.

"No…no, that's not it at all. It's not the crossing, or actually walking on hot coals that scorched their feet. It's the deal they made. Don't you see? This so called 'coyote' is a liar and when he speaks a lie, he speaks from his own nature, because he is a liar.[22] Everyone knows this…you can't blame education, upbringing or even that these people may or may not be in a desperate situation. These dreadful people aren't ignorant of the coyote's schemes,[23]" proclaimed Mr. Carlisle. Once again, I was bothered by this victim blaming. I was no bleeding heart sympathizer by any means, but there comes a point of desperation for anyone, where they can be had, and I said as much to him.

---

[22] John 8:44
[23] 2 Cor. 2:10-11

Mr. Carlisle smiled and asked, "What's your point of desperation? Hmmm? When you reach that point of desperation…are you given carte blanche to do anything you want?"

"No, I'm saying a person makes poor decisions when in desperate situation, and we shouldn't blame them for having a lapse in judgment."

"Can you kill a man? You know…because of poor judgment?" I didn't answer. My face was hot with embarrassment as Mr. Carlisle had boxed me in a corner on this and clearly he would continue to do so on such hot button issues. I smiled and nodded, acknowledging he had beat me, but not giving him the satisfaction of an actual official acknowledgement. For all practical purposes, he still didn't make any sense. Killing someone was quite different than trusting someone, which is what these people did, they just trusted the wrong bad guy to get them across.

"Maybe the coyote was in a desperate situation? Maybe if he didn't do this task, the cartel would kill his family or him. Or maybe he needed the money to feed his family. Is it wrong to kill one person to save a whole family? Isn't what those migrants did a form of greed? They could have said no to this ridiculous deal if they wanted, but they had money on their hearts and they wanted to get across now instead of when they were supposed to go across," concluded Mr. Carlisle. I knew there was no convincing him of any other perspective. I was not going to play along anymore. I was going to finish my steak.

However, his arguments lingered in my mind. I began to question my cut and dry moral reasoning and I couldn't determine if I was already confused and Mr. Carlisle was just shedding light on my confusion or if Mr. Carlisle himself was causing the confusion. Maybe I didn't even understand all the moral and ethical perspectives in the world as much as I originally thought. Life's ethical and moral concerns should be black and white…there should be no confusion.

Rarely, up until that particular point in my life, did I make a moral decision that took longer than twenty seconds to decide. I was always completely sure of myself and thus confident to address arguments presented by someone else such as Mr. Carlisle. Unfortunately, it seemed like Mr. Carlisle had a vast amount of superior knowledge and experience than me. I had lost confidence in my ability to ascertain a moral conclusion and Mr. Carlisle's apparent wisdom seemed to rob me of my confidence and thus question the moral lines I had so easily drawn in the past. I could read and hear the moral doctrines, but if I truly didn't understand them, then Mr. Carlisle could easily snatch away whatever moral boundaries I had already had in place within my mind.[24]

We sat there, uncomfortably eating for a time, at least I was uncomfortable as Mr. Carlisle seemed absolutely content with how we ended our conversation. He must have sensed something was wrong with me because he smiled gently and broke the silence, "Look, there's a reason the firm chose you for this task. They believe in you and obviously feel like you're more capable than anyone else to handle the situation. Why else would they send you down here? By the way, if they value you this much, you're probably being undervalued as far as compensation goes. If I were you, I'd probably try and leverage a bigger bonus this year."

"Not sure I have the leverage for that...I mean, this is a financial loss. I'll be behind on my hours. I don't see how you could leverage this into more money," I responded.

Mr. Carlisle sighed, "You don't have the leverage because of the free legal work; you have leverage because they think highly enough of you to handle this situation. It costs money to replace good associates, you're not doing something that can easily be replaced. You are unique to the firm and unique things are valued higher than common things."

---

[24] Matt 13:9

With that, the conversation turned to lighter fare, such as Mr. Carlisle's travels, which were extensive and he told me tales of the important people he interacted with, which was also an extensive list.

All and all, it was an enjoyable evening. I headed back to my hotel in order to get some sleep before my meeting with the Judge and possibly the Prosecutor. Admittedly, I fantasized a bit about walking into the managing partner's office and negotiating for more money. I fell asleep imagining friends, family and colleagues toasting me for some unknown reason.

Chapter 4 – The Briefcase.

I woke up early to get a jump on the day. I wanted to make sure I was presentable to the Judge and Prosecutor. I had never met these gentlemen before and I wanted them to know that I was taking this seriously and to represent my firm in the best possible way. I assumed that they didn't get a lot of big firm interest in their area unless there was some sort of class action products liability claim or something similar. I wanted them to know that I would give it my all, even for a pro bono matter.

I was certain that my knowledge of the law was superior given the reputation of my law school and firm. I already knew some of the pitfalls of practicing law in south Texas as told by some of my colleagues. If you're not local, you will likely lose your hearing or trial because you are not a voter and the Judge will likely never see you again. In order to win a case down there, you had to hire a local attorney and even that was no guarantee. It was a close knit community and as much as they protect their own, they also held grudges against each other. Still, you had a better shot of winning if you had a local on your team than if you didn't. I felt like this situation was different though, as I was doing charity work and not going up against anyone in particular that had an interest in the community.

After my grooming and preparation, I headed down to see if the complimentary breakfast buffet was started…it was and it excited me. I gorged on eggs, hash browns, sausage and bacon. These items are not available at home, so I felt no guilt in my gluttonous behavior. My mindset was one of a person that may or may not eat this food again. These weren't high quality delicacies, but I wanted them and lots of them. I ate until I was in pain, which was the only reason I stopped. It was a good thing, because I needed to get on with my day.

I checked with the front desk to see if Mr. Carlisle had my legal briefing dropped off and it was. I took the briefcase up to my room, placed in on the bed so I could review the briefing before giving it to the Judge. I didn't want to sound like an idiot, so I thought I would get familiarized with the legal work before we discussed the matter. I assumed it would be about immigration or criminal law, both of which were not my strong suits, but I was confident enough in my abilities to be competent for our meeting at least.

Unfortunately, my quest to be prepared was thwarted by the fact that someone actually used the lock on the briefcase. I've carried around a briefcase with a lock on it for as long as I can remember, yet I don't recall ever having a time where I felt it necessary to lock the briefcase. I assumed that because the briefing was left with the front desk, the firm didn't want to risk any confidential communique getting out there. I had no idea the combination, so I phoned in to work to see if anyone had a clue. My secretary didn't even know I was gone and absolutely had no idea who worked on this matter. I told her to find out what she could and let me know.

She never called me back. If I didn't leave soon, I'd be late for my meeting, which would be worse than showing a bit of legal ignorance. I would just need to meet the Judge and Prosecutor and let them know that I would retrieve the combination as soon as possible. It was embarrassing, but better than standing them up.

I arrived at the courthouse, passed through the metal detectors and made my way up to the Judge's courtroom. When I asked the Bailiff to see the Judge, he nodded and escorted me quickly over to the Prosecutor's table. I found this to be strange, but it was the first time I'd been in the court, so who's to know for sure how this judge runs things?

I put the briefcase in front of the Prosecutor and was about to explain that I didn't know the combination to the lock, when he stood up and motioned me to follow him outside the courtroom. He led me down the hall to his office, took the briefcase from me, put it behind the desk and gave me a bag from a fast food restaurant.

The Prosecutor could immediately see that I was confused and explained, "Thanks for the briefing, take the Judge his burger and fries for me would you? You can just go straight up to him during the proceedings, he doesn't care. He gets hungry and doesn't want to stop his docket if he's running late, which it always is because we handle criminal, civil, family and probate matters all together. We're not specialized like the larger districts. Oh, and don't open his lunch bag. He hates that…he thinks someone is eating his fries. Just keep it tight like it comes from the drive-through. Thanks."

Still puzzled, I was about to try again to mention to him that the briefcase was locked when he entered the combination and opened it before I could get a word out. I was still standing over him, stunned actually, but also wanting to get a peek inside the case as I was curious as to the briefing. The Prosecutor barely opened the case in my presence, and I only saw a name on the top of a page, "Robin Keller" is all it said. Robin Keller must have been a party in some sort of case law that was on point.

Within a few seconds, the Prosecutor looked up silently in a manner that suggested that I should leave. I obliged and left with the burgers, assuming that our firm is lending him our briefcase, which seemed unnecessary for a pro-bono matter. I never questioned providing free legal work, that was part of our duty, part of the oath, but it doesn't mean that we need to just let people use our high end briefcases. By the time we would get them back, the normal wear and tear alone will diminish its value. Besides, people often treat company property poorly, especially if it's from another company or firm. That's why rental cars always stink and have scratches all over them. Nobody minds running over a curb in a rental car.

While the briefcase issue bothered me, it was the fact that the Prosecutor barely acknowledged me that was really irritating me. Here we were, helping him out and he didn't even introduce himself, I didn't even know his name. He just took our work and made me a delivery boy to the Judge. We weren't making money off this, we were helping people and he didn't seem to care. It was almost like I was a burden. To top it off, I was an attorney at a prestigious firm and I had to parade in front of everyone, attorneys included, and delivering fast food to a judge! I wanted to meet the Judge of course, the more contacts you have in the judiciary the better, but this was not what I had in mind. First impressions are lasting and I would be known to the Judge as the delivery boy, not a colleague and not a heavy hitting attorney, just a guy bringing him his stupid burgers.

I was at least owed a French fry out of this. I took the burger bag back to my rental car, so nobody could see me. I opened the bag, pushed the burger out of the way to get a fry and found a small stack of cash. I closed the bag and looked away. My stomach dropped, I immediately began to sweat. Without thinking, I turned the key and drove out of the parking lot and several blocks from the courthouse. Good Lord, I hoped nobody had noticed me.

I pulled over, looked in the bag again to confirm and sure enough, there was cash. This was really bad! Really bad. They were having me bribe the Judge.

I couldn't go through with it. This was a black and white issue…absolutely no gray area. You bribe a judge, you are a criminal and shall remain a criminal. Then what's next? Once you take a step down that road you basically have two paths; you continue with your life as somebody with no morals or you have your mea culpa, which will bring down you and everyone and thing you love in the process. Either way, your life as you know it will never be the same. If anyone knows the good they ought to do and doesn't do it, it is sin for them.[25]

If a person were to cross that moral and ethical line, which is a major crossing as it is not like rolling through a stop sign, the likelihood of a mea culpa seems rather far fetched. As a hypothetical, if I were to have delivered the cash as suggested, then I would automatically be tied with at a minimum two other criminals for life. Two other people with low moral standards, two potentially dangerous people would be linked to me and be a part of my life until I died. That was just the Judge and Prosecutor. There was a strong possibility that Mr. Carlisle knew of the matter and was in on it, in addition to whoever was actually doing the bribing, assuming that Mr. Carlisle was just the middle man. So, once I completed the bribe, I would be with two or more criminals and once a person is surrounded by those with low moral standards, then such behavior is encouraged and justified until one day you are face down in the filth of the world without even knowing it. You've got to keep a good reputation even with those outside your circle, so that you won't fall into reproach and the snare of those that are filth.[26]

If your morals slip and you surround yourself with people whose morals are just as loose, then there is no perceived judgment and a sort of desensitization takes place. Evil men and imposters will proceed from bad to worse, deceiving and being deceived.[27]

For example, I enjoyed cold showers in the morning, it would get my blood flowing and I believed it was probably better for my skin because it wouldn't dry it out. At one time, I did not like cold showers. I gradually reduced the shower temperature every day until I was used to the cold temperature, then preferred the cold temperature and then never wanted to return to a hot shower. That was how morality worked. You sin, surround yourself with sinners, justify your sins, sin with others in greater volume and get to a point where you don't want to return. We all,

---

[25] Jas 4:17
[26] 1 Tim. 3:7
[27] 2 Tim. 3:13

like sheep, have gone astray, each of us at some point has turned to our own way.[28] Even if you wanted to return to a moral lifestyle, the jolt of such a return seemed too traumatic for many to want to undertake. The gradual and gentle method that takes a person to immorality will not be the method of return from it. The transition will be a harsh slap in the face…from a person's own design or from beyond control, but that person will be slapped.

One has to serve somebody or something and it's best to keep it clean. I did not have a spirit of timidity, but a spirit of power, of love and self-discipline![29] There was no decision to be made about whether I would go through with this nasty act.

While it seemed like several hours, I really only thought about the scenario for a couple of minutes then immediately started the car and went back to the hotel room. I put the money on my bed and stared at it. I never counted it, never knew the exact amount, but it was enough to make someone change his mind or make sure he didn't.

Soon, a bigger question loomed. Whether to bribe or not was an easy question to answer, I would never bribe somebody or knowingly be a part of such a situation, but then what? Would I turn it into the police, FBI, take it back to the firm and report it to them…what was I to do?

The compadre system…that's what some of the locals called it. It would be shocking to those from outside the region, those that sit daintily on high horses, but in south Texas, it was not particularly an outrageous system. For many in fact, it was a necessary way of doing business. All one needed to do was watch the local news and you could see it taking place in all jurisdictions and all levels. This included federal, state, county, city, law enforcement, judicial, jails, prosecution, representatives all the way to the school board.

---

[28] Isa 53:6
[29] 2 Tim 1:7

I remember reading about a school board trustee who was indicted on wire fraud. A school board trustee! It was about fake bids for projects for work, products and services provided for the school district. It was a big district, but this trustee had his hands in everything or at least a cousin or in-law did. Construction projects, food services, security, special needs experts, healthcare plans…everything a school district needed this trustee was somehow involved. The compadre system. If it wasn't the trustee that received a piece of the action, he certainly made sure it was someone he knew. The compadre system. Get all the relatives and friends involved so nobody rats each other out.

A lot of them got caught though, like that trustee. It was likely that he didn't grease the right wheels or cut someone out. So then it goes down the line. How aggressive will the prosecution be if he gets a little cash bonus this time around? What about the Judge?

Then there was the drugs and other trafficking. I saw somewhere that ninety percent of cocaine brought into the states comes in through Mexico. That's a big percentage, which means there's a lot of people that have an interest at stake. It wasn't just local trustees caught up in this underground economy. I saw somewhere that over a ten year period, almost two hundred employees and contract workers of the Department of Homeland Security took nearly fifteen million dollars in bribes while being paid to protect the border and enforce the law. This could mean that green cards were illegally sold or that sensitive information could be purchased by the cartels. Customs and Border Protection officers and Border Patrol agents have been caught taking bribes to help smuggle drugs into the country. Sometimes a headless body is found and things get traced back to those who are employed to protect.

Full sheriff department units have been thrown in prison for corruption. Then, just a few years later the same department gets busted again. It was the same corruption, the same problems only the second time it was perpetrated by a different family member. For the local jurisdictions, it was a family business.

If the Judge and Prosecutor were on the take then local police was out of the question. While I'm sure not all the local law enforcement officers were part of the corruption, at least a few were and were willing to protect themselves and others involved. It had to be the FBI. I needed to take the local flavor out of the matter and let the feds take over. The federal prosecutor would be the one going after the Judge and local prosecutor anyway, other than an internal audit, which would seem farfetched. That would be my only choice. Give it to the FBI and get out of the way. I sighed in relief. I hated not having an answer or a plan in place. I hated drifting. I always needed a target. I needed to go to the FBI and I would do so immediately.

At that very moment, my phone rang. Not my cell phone, my room line. I didn't even know people called the phones in the hotel rooms anymore. It was the front desk telling me I had a visitor in the lobby. I was nervous. I had no idea who would be calling on me. If they knew me, they would have my cell phone. It must be law enforcement. Hopefully the FBI were already tracking this and wanted to talk to me. It was still nerve wracking. I didn't do anything wrong, so why should I be nervous? What if they thought I did something criminal? What if the bad guys were coming after me? I didn't do anything wrong. There was nothing to be nervous about.

I cautiously came down to the lobby, hoping to catch a glimpse of my visitor in order to prepare myself before I approached. It was Mr. Carlisle. He was looking right at me, our eyes met and the meeting was unavoidable. He stood up and motioned for me to sit down across from him. He smiled and didn't seem angry, which was surprising given the fact that I stood up a judge. I assumed he would be furious once he found out I didn't deliver the money. Maybe Mr. Carlisle didn't know about it or maybe he didn't even know anything and he was just as innocent as me.

"Sounds like you had second thoughts about the delivery," inquired Mr. Carlisle.

"The briefcase? No I delivered it and the Prosecutor kept the briefcase by the way. I thought you should know," I replied.

"Nope...I'm talking about the money. It sounds like you forgot to give it to the Judge."

"I didn't forget. I decided not to bribe a judge, that's all. You can't bribe a judge. Quite frankly, it was an easy decision," I said firmly. I wasn't going to back down on this one, there was no justification to go through with it. Mr. Carlisle shook his head and smiled, as if he knew something I didn't.

"That's fine, kid. Do what you want. I'm sure you're assuming you made the right decision," responded Mr. Carlisle. He paused for a second, looked up at the ceiling and then continued, "I know what's right and wrong, most of us do anyway. I know that you bribing a judge is wrong..."

"I didn't bribe a judge or even attempt to bribe a judge, you did!" I interrupted.

"Nope, you did. I've got nothing to do with this. I gave you legal briefing. I never touched any money or discussed you bribing anybody. You came up with that on your own. I've never been a part of this little scheme...although you were directly involved, weren't you? Anyway, none of this matters anymore. You made the decision not to deliver the money to the Judge. It was your decision and you made it. So now you're on a path and you can't go back. Whatever organization is behind this little scheme will come for you. They will come for you and your family or...maybe just your family, they like to do that just to make sure you live long enough to feel the most pain you can possibly feel. Monetarily, this is a minor incident. The amount of money you were supposed to deliver is inconsequential to a multi-billion dollar operation. But these organizations…they don't take insubordination lightly. They can't maintain their operation at that level if there is a perception that one doesn't need to listen or follow directions. So, insubordination will result in retribution, no matter how small of a matter. An American lawyer who was supposed to deliver a bribe to an official, but doesn't…that's you, will be severely and publicly punished in order to maintain order. If they do awful things to your family, then you will talk about it, be put on television blubbering about how you miss them and how you want justice. Everyone will see what happens to insubordinates," concluded Mr. Carlisle as he sat back in his chair to let me digest his words.

I was scared and livid. "What's wrong with you? Why did you do this to me?" my voice was growing louder.

Mr. Carlisle smirked, "I did nothing. You chose to accept the assignment without question. Why were you chosen to undertake such a task? Because you are such a great lawyer? You're not a blip on the radar. I did nothing to you. You could have just delivered the money without looking in the bag. Nothing would have happened and you wouldn't even have known you did anything wrong. What makes you a hero? You're no different than anyone else, why do you think you can derail this whole thing and make a difference? You think you're without fault? The deeds of some men are conspicuous, going before them to judgment, but the deeds of others, like yourself appear later.[30]"

"Then take the money from me and deliver it yourself," I suggested.

---

[30] 1 Tim. 5:24

"No, my work is done. This is on you now. Nothing traces me to this, it's all on you. I will still go on doing what I do. You...you will not. Even if things work out for you and you are able to do what you consider the 'right thing', your life as you know it is over. If nothing happens to you, and that's a big if, you will always be looking over your shoulder...knowing that this is bigger than what your little brain can perceive...knowing that there are far worse elements involved than just a simple transaction...knowing that you set off a chain reaction of badness that may come down on you or your innocent loved ones at any time. No, I will not help you, nor could I help you if I wanted. After that stupid split second of thought you put into this, you brought forth a plague. You think you have the right to cause people to die? What harm did that judge do to you? Every now and then he takes a few bucks here and there. He's a public figure elected by the people because they believed he could make the right decisions or judge if you will. You don't know how many times he's done this, nor how many people he's kept safe by playing ball with this group. Maybe a few immigrants' lives get lost every now and then, maybe the organization oversteps its bounds a bit, but maybe that judge and prosecutor helped keep things a little less violent by looking away every now and then. Maybe by looking the other way every now and then, those government officials keep our own citizens just a bit more safe. That judge and prosecutor might be dead at this very moment because of you," explained Mr. Carlisle, as he tried to convince me that he himself was an angel of light.[31]

Every person must face a dilemma. If you live long enough, you come to a point where you need to make a major decision. We can all come up with scenarios in our mind of great challenges...cancer, car wrecks, loss of employment, violence or all sorts of other scenes in which we must rise up to become a hero or just cower away. We come up with ways to handle

---

[31] 2 Cor. 11:14

those situations, the right ways. Unfortunately, the problems most people actually end up facing and are the most difficult, are often the ones they don't anticipate. That's how one becomes refined, tested and it's determined what kind of core person they are at the time of crisis.

So here I was. Once again, there was no question I was doing the moral and ethical thing by going to the feds. No question. However, was it the right thing? Was I willing to put my family in danger? Given Mr. Carlisle's assertion that the damage was already done, I believed that my choice was made, so there was no backing out of it. I needed to contact the FBI, tell them that I believed my family was in danger and go from there. I needed to hurry.

I excused myself from Mr. Carlisle, he didn't seem to care, and made my way back to my room. Housekeeping must have come in because my bed was made. This gave me pause. A jump in my stomach. Someone had been in my room. Were they still there? Were things moved?

I did not see the money nor the fast food bag! Gone. I couldn't breathe. I knew it was gone for good before I even tore apart the room looking for it. It was gone! If it was the housekeeper, I'm guessing she took the cash, hopped on a bus and was it was lost forever. Whatever the amount of cash, it was enough to quit being a housekeeper for the rest of her life.

I yelled into my pillow and I'll admit that I sobbed for a bit, as quietly as possible. I wondered what I could do now. I shouted out in desperation to be shown a way, to be taught a path, and to be guided in truth.[32] What could I possibly say to the FBI? I gave a briefcase to the Prosecutor, who gave me a bag of cash to give to a judge, but the cash is missing. It's just an accusation. That's all I had, just an accusation. A second year attorney from out of town is accusing a prosecutor and judge of corruption with absolutely no evidence. I didn't know their

---

[32] Psa. 25:4-5

names, I didn't even have the briefcase! Why would anybody offer me protection or for my family for that matter? What good would come of it? I've got nothing to offer, no leverage, and no incentive to do anything. In an instant, I become another person randomly making an accusation against a government official. That's what it would be, a random accusation against two unnamed individuals and a Mr. Carlisle, who did nothing and whose first name is unknown to me as well! How? How was I in a situation where every single aspect was against me?

I needed to figure out why I of all people was connected to this matter. Why was I chosen to give a bribe to a judge? Was I being tested and would I come forth as gold?[33] If this was a routine bribe that took place every month or two, wouldn't the bad guys use someone they knew or trusted? Why would they choose a random lawyer? None of it made sense. I was asked to come down and handle pro bono work for some illegal immigrants who were victims of a terrible tragedy. Then all of a sudden, one of the victims dies, the same victim I was set to represent and then I am asked to deliver some briefing to the Judge and Prosecutor associated with the matter, which in turn ended up being some form of bribery. I couldn't wrap my mind around this convoluted matter.

If I remained disciplined, would I be chastened?[34] I had to keep myself together. If I were to panic, then even worse decisions would be made.

I determined that these events couldn't be mere coincidences. Somehow there must be a connection to the attack on the migrants and my bribery situation. I wasn't sure if there was a direct connection, but the two situations must be related in some form. Otherwise, I would have been too random of a target for this type of deal. So I was dealing with murder, attempted murder and bribery. That's all.

---

[33] Job 23:10
[34] Heb. 12:6

This was the moment when I became overcome with a special kind of dread. This was not the dread that you feel when you hear a sound coming from behind a door and you are afraid to open it because you don't know what's on the other side. No, this was a dread associated with the impending doom. You know what is on the other side of the door. In other words, I knew something terrible is going to happen no matter which choice I made from that point forward and there was nothing I could do about it. I didn't know who the bad guys were, but I knew they could move swiftly. The question was, should I move my family and cause my wife panic or was I just too small of a concern for the bad guys to do anything towards me? Thinking back, I didn't remember giving the Prosecutor my name or any information for that matter. However, if there was some sort of arrangement with Mr. Carlisle, then the Prosecutor and Judge had to have known my identity. I doubt Mr. Carlisle would have made arrangements without telling anybody who I was or at least that I worked for my firm.

I decided that out of an abundance of caution, I should call my wife. I paced around the room a bit, trying to gather the story in a way that wouldn't cause an absolute panic, but that seemed like a tall order. I called her and partially explained the situation. I told her that this pro bono work might include some bad characters and that she should be extra careful, maybe go visit her parents with the kids for a few days. She did not take this well at all. She wanted to call the police of course, but if she called our local police, they would call the local police down here and I may be dealing with another person who might be part of the whole conspiracy. It was a logical assumption. My wife took this news much worse. I told her that the FBI would be the way to go as they don't have local ties and she seemed to agree with me on that regard. I talked to the kids for a bit, not too much as to arouse concern or suspicion. I kept it light, but on my end it was a form of goodbye. My wife and I had a bit of a sob, I assured her that things would quickly get back to normal when everything was resolved and we hung up. I sobbed again. I'm sure she did as well.

Now that my wife was informed and hopefully safe sooner rather than later, I had to confront the task of how I was going to proceed. I was sure that my wife would try and talk to the FBI, but luckily she would run into the same issue I was faced with about evidence and nobody actually doing anything against the law, yet. They would be polite with her and then ignore her, which was what they would likely do with me. So, I decided to do the only thing a man who was facing impending doom was able to do; I needed to have company. It's not good that I should be alone, I needed a helper fit for me.[35] I needed to talk to someone else I knew was also involved in this matter whether they liked it or not. I needed to see that game warden that witnessed the whole damn mess at the river.

---

[35] Gen. 2:18

Chapter 5 – The Game Warden.

It would be virtually impossible to determine which local officers I could turn to in order to discuss either the immigrant or the bribery situation. I had no way of knowing which ones I could trust. The FBI, Secret Service, Border Patrol or any other federal entity would have no reason to discuss anything with a civilian who had nothing more than a blanket allegation against two local officials.

I knew that a game warden had witnessed the attempted crossing and burning of the migrants. I also knew that the Game Warden was female from my discussions with Mr. Carlisle. I lacked knowledge of her actual name because the papers and local news referenced most of the officials and witnesses involved in generalities instead of giving specific names. In other words, the news would state, "Local game warden witnesses act of atrocity," and leave it at that. Given the shocking nature of it all, the media covered the matter extensively, but with little detail. I assumed the news didn't go into the names of those involved, other than the heads of the departments, in order to protect those with knowledge. If the Game Warden ended up with her head lopped off in the desert somewhere, the local news producer would have some difficulty getting to sleep for a few days. It turned out that their half-hearted attempt to protect the names of the witnesses was pointless. I could easily count the number of female game wardens in Texas on one hand and could count the number of female game wardens in the Rio Grande Valley on one finger. It was an easy numbers game.

"This is Robin Keller," the Game Warden said over the phone. My stomach tightened a bit when I heard that name. I knew that name. She was on the paper I saw from the briefcase. It wasn't legal briefing. Whatever I gave to the bad guys included her name. Was it part of a witness list? Was it an order to do something about her? I couldn't figure out for sure the significance of it all, other than the fact that it was likely not a good thing to be named in those papers. Especially when the briefcase was exchanged.

I managed to regain my composure a bit to explain to Robin that I was working on a pro bono matter involving the border crossers she witnessed being attacked. I left out the other issues for the moment. She agreed to meet me after her day was done over at a local diner. Robin seemed like she really wanted to let me know what she witnessed, assuming it would help with my representation of the victims. I had a feeling that having seen the horrors of it all, she wanted to make sure these people were in good hands.

As the day ended, I headed over to the diner where she suggested we meet, thinking the whole way about the totality of my situation. Did I want more knowledge about it all? Wouldn't ignorance be the better course of action? I knew that I wasn't supposed to participate in the unfruitful deeds of darkness, but instead I was to expose them.[36] But could I? In the end, it wouldn't matter. I had lost a bribe and my actions signaled to the powers that be that I was not going to cooperate with them. This meant that I needed to be silenced. It was a matter of time now. I needed to know what happened and how exactly I fit into the scheme of things before I got help. Most importantly, I needed to know who I could trust to help me.

"This was a bad scene," the Robin said gravely, "I've never come across anything like it before and I hope never again. That smell of burning hair is still in my nose. I can't get rid of it. I burned something in the oven the other day and it…it made me remember it all. It made me sick to my stomach." Her blue eyes were wide open as she began, as if she was watching the whole thing play out again in real time. She took a sip of her iced tea and pause for a moment, presumably to gather herself.

---

[36] Eph. 5:11

"I was on the opposite bank. I normally never hear anything or see anything when it happens…someone crossing. They do it at night, long after my shift. I'll see shirts or water bottles the next day every once and awhile, but nobody ever crosses when I'm there. It was weird. Why would anyone cross when it's still daylight?" Robin looked down at the counter for a bit, seemingly transporting herself back to that moment in time.

"They did it around dusk, so why not wait until after midnight sometime? It just doesn't sit well, the whole thing. I've ended my day at the same spot for the last two years. I sit on that bank, have a snack and a bottle of water, and then go home. When the sun starts getting low, that's when the birds come to hunt for fish and the fish come out to hunt for bugs and so on. That's when life wakes up. That's when I get to see the beauty of the river. I enjoy unwinding and observing the action. Most of my days are pretty uneventful, so this is the time when I get to see life going through its cycle. I didn't know I would get it the way I did," Robin sat back and looked at me with a bit of relief, as if she found a kindred spirit of sorts.

Maybe she was struggling with the similar issues as me about who to trust? I thought it doubtful as all she did was witness the aftermath, while I was actually embroiled and potentially able to be implicated in the whole affair. Maybe it was a fish out of water factor. She was fair skinned and red haired, a rare combination in these parts. The fact that she was a woman game warden was extremely unusual. She was alone in a sense, small and slight amongst large and boastful.

Robin continued, "Like I said, it was a strange occurrence. I sat there, eating my snack…I think a bag of grapes or something, and then I started hearing men's voices. Loud, clearly not hiding from anything. It's not like they're breaking the law by being loud on the Mexican side of the river, but I'd just never heard any voices before. If anybody is on the other side, they generally don't want to be discovered, so I'm told. I mean...I've never seen a human being on the other side of that bank...in two years. Just remnants from the night before. So I hear these men, I don't really see them, but they are loud enough to cause me to pull out my binoculars to take a look. I saw nothing but outlines or glimpses of them walking around in the scrub over there. There are clumps of brush and bushes, basically the only cover you would have. They stayed under cover, but they kept it loud. I don't know. Maybe they were drunk or just didn't care. These were beefier men, they weren't the ones crossing over, so maybe they just didn't care. If they weren't crossing, what do they care if people heard them?"

The waitress came by and took our order, Robin pointed at something on the menu. I noticed that her hands were slight, like a doll's. She went on, "The whole thing had an eerie vibe to it. I'm sitting there listening to these guys horsing around, watching what I could and then it just got real quiet. Normally, I would have left to go home by then, but within about fifteen minutes I heard some splashing just a few yards downstream. It was beginning to get a little dark, but it was bright enough to see a group of people getting in one of those inflatable rafts to cross the river. They were packed in there tight. I thought they would sink immediately, but somehow they kept the thing afloat. They were so packed in there that all sort of splashing and bickering was going on...nobody could have snuck over like that. I sat there kind of stunned for a while, I had been trained and told about crossers, but I had never seen it. It's like you prepare for an emergency or an incident, but you have that bit of a pause when it actually happens...like your feet are in mud. Anyway, I called it in. Technically, I can detain people, as I'm law enforcement, but really...I would have been overrun. Who knows what would have happened? These people that cross are pretty desperate, so it's probably best not to have a five foot two woman take on a raft of illegal immigrants by herself. I wouldn't know what to do with them if I

54

caught them anyway. They've seen far worse than me to get to this point, so it was best that I called it in. Dispatch would relay the message over to border patrol or the local boys. My duty was to stay put and make sure I didn't lose visual contact. Well, they got about half way across and then it happened."

Robin paused, took a sip of water and then just went into it, "The whole thing went up like a fireball. I know something was thrown from the Mexican bank that landed in the raft. Something that set the whole thing off. I've never seen something go up in flames that fast, that big. I mean…nobody could have gotten out of there without getting burned. I called in for first responders now. The situation had changed. These people weren't going to make it. Just screams, bodies wriggling…like you see a rabbit after being shot…just wriggling around all on top of each other. Screaming, lots of screaming. The river glowed orange. I could feel a wall of heat from where I was standing on the bank, which was several yards back. I couldn't imagine…just your skin melting."

Robin sighed, looked down at hands, then here phone awkwardly, waited a few minutes and said, "We were just dragging folks out of the river. Skin fried, hair burnt. Just the looks of terror on their faces. They were clinging on me, laying down and just reaching up, grabbing my shirt, pulling me down to them. Just screaming things in Spanish. I didn't know what they were saying. I know a bit, that's what got me the job down here, but not like this. They were just screaming things I couldn't understand." She turned her head sharply, as if she wanted to hide her face from me, dabbing her eyes a bit with a napkin. I could see that she was done reliving it all. She cleared her throat and indicated that she was done with the discussion.

A South Texas parks and wildlife region may have as many as three game wardens patrolling three thousand square miles divided up between them. One game warden may cover two hundred to four hundred miles a day, alone. Primarily, one becomes a game warden for the sake of conservation. A game warden's main job is to prevent poaching, basically enforcing the state's hunting and fishing laws. Technically, a game warden is a peace officer charged with enforcing all of the state's criminal laws. This latter part of the job duties has been increasing over the years as drug cartels have become ever more emboldened.

The likelihood of a Texas game warden being killed in the line of duty is still relatively rare as these are highly trained individuals blessed with temperaments to deal with a variety of different people and are generally dealing with cooperative individuals. The chance of being hurt or killed by someone involved in the drug or human trafficking trade is even rarer as most of a game warden's dangerous encounters are with drunk or startled poachers. However, the element of such a new danger is real. Every now and then news comes of a park ranger stumbling onto a cartel's marijuana crop or narcotics stash in a national or state park. Wherever a cartel has product, there are guards and these guards are paid to kill upon discovery. If a park ranger or game warden sees a stash, they must be killed or the operation is over and people lose money...lots of money.

As a game warden, whose territory covers portions of the Rio Grande, Robin explained that she had been briefed and was fully aware that she more likely than not would run into an act of human or drug smuggling at some point in time in her career. As she had explained to me, every now and then she would come across some remnants of an illegal border crossing, either a water bottle, a shoe or some other article left behind during the crossing. She guessed that those responsible for illegal activity could easily keep an eye on her, while she would just be chasing ghosts, which is how Robin preferred it. She wanted to be seen and had no desire to stumble into a smuggling in process. Her goal was to protect wildlife, and people if she had to, but mainly wildlife. Besides, those on the other side of the border had no respect for her authority, they just knew it was wiser not to be discovered by any government official. Robin knew that if confronted, they would not hesitate to take her out of the picture.

Robin was the only female game warden in southern Texas. At five foot two, the fair skinned redhead always had to overcome her size and appearance with mental toughness and a relentless character. She's confronted two hundred and sixty pound men with guns. Men who were angry at what she had to say. One time she even used a fireman's carry on a lone hunter who fell from a deer stand and broke his leg. She used balance and leverage to bring him out of the woods to safety. The hunter surely doubted her capabilities, but like everyone else who ever doubted Robin, she changed his mind and he was grateful.

Robin loved the outdoors and grew up on the other side of the state in East Texas as a tomboy hunting and fishing with her dad and brothers. While most little girls in Texas knew of hunting and knew that whitetail season meant that daddy was gone a bunch, few enjoyed to participating in the hunt like Robin did. Robin was up for anything, in the spring, she would start bass fishing, if they weren't biting, she would fish for catfish. In the fall, Robin would hunt anything and everything she could. If hunting season was over, she would be perfectly content just being in the thick pine tree forests. Back then, there were miles of trees around her when she ventured in the woods and it was always quiet, the trees blocked the sound from the outside world.

Growing up the way she did, Robin felt like becoming a game warden was her true calling in life. Once she finished training and was offered a spot, she immediately accepted without regard for the location. It took some time to get used to it, but the valley has grown in her and she has come to think of it as home. She especially loved her patrol area. It was a rugged countryside, scrub brush being the main landscape. She could actually see a horizon, which was not the case when she lived in the piney woods.

Sitting there across from me, I could sense that a part of Robin wished she was back in those piney woods. She was alone, but not safe. She didn't want to be a part of that horrible scene, but she was. I think that's why she opened up to me. She was done being interviewed by law enforcement and nobody back home really understood the situation. She was lacking confidence. One should never throw away confidence, which has a great reward.[37] Here I was, somebody presumably sent to help these people out and Robin must have felt a bit of a kindred spirit, someone else in the muck with her, which was my motivation as well. That was not the entire scope of it, though. Here was this person who clearly felt scared and vulnerable and I had the knowledge that the bad guys had a piece of paper with her name on it. What good would it do to tell her? It's not like they couldn't have found her name without it. She's the only female game warden in Texas and was an eye witness to the tragedy. They didn't need any special information to track her down, here whereabouts would be easily known. Heck, I found her myself. If I told her about the paper, it would just cause more unnecessary panic and might even prompt her to go to the wrong law enforcement for help. Then she'd have real problems. No, she would get over this soon enough. I needed more information though.

"Do you know anyone else that saw anything?" I asked.

"Nobody saw what I saw, which is good for them….but I got a strange call from a deputy the other day. I didn't return his call because I found out he was suspended or on leave…whatever you call it. He just left me a message asking me to give him a call. I haven't bothered, assuming he's a bit sketchy given his suspension," explained Robin.

---

[37] Heb. 10:35

58

"Why was he suspended?" I asked.

"Don't know. I just think it wise to stay away from a suspended officer, don't you? I mean, what good could come from it?" asked Robin. We finished up and bid goodbye. Before we parted ways, I asked for the deputy's information. She said, "Rudy Garza."

"Rudy Garza?" I asked.

"Yep, everyone has two first names down here. It's probably legally Rudolpho," with that, Robin waived and was on her way.

It seemed like this was all the information I was going to get out of Robin. She witnessed the attack, but did not see the attackers and had no way of knowing the identity of anyone involved. The incident was chaotic and horrific and Robin was in no position to gain any information as to anyone involved as she was merely trying to save lives. But what about this deputy? Was he just trying to fish around to find out what Robin knew? If he was suspended, was it because he knew the truth and was trying to do the right thing or was it because he was just as corrupt as the others and was beings suspended for some misdeeds? Was he the one that gathered names, the same names I delivered? Any meeting with this Rudy Garza seemed like it could go very wrong if his motivations were less than stellar.

So, was my desire to get to the bottom of the matter greater than my aversion to risk? That's what I needed to determine. Was my ultimate gain in all this to provide safety for my family, do the right thing, end it all or did I just want to get answers for my own edification? I was deceiving myself if I thought I knew the answers. Let no one deceive himself…I needed to become a fool so that I might become wise.[38] No matter my motivation or desired ends, I needed

---

[38] 1 Cor. 3:18

to meet with Deputy Garza, otherwise I'd be left wondering where it all led and where it was going. I needed answers. I needed truth.

Chapter 6 – Have a Cigar.

I decided to head back to the hotel for the evening; I'd pick up a meal at the restaurant there as I was in no mood to go out. Obviously, a hotel restaurant would be hit and miss. I've been to some that are destinations, regardless of whether or not you are staying there and others that thaw out whatever you want to eat and charge you double for a piece of rubber to chew on for a half an hour or so until you spit it out, pay your bill and go to bed! If I were to put it on my room tab it would be more palatable to eat terrible food for high prices because I was mixing it in with another preexisting outrageous bill.

Sometimes I just wanted to fill my stomach and I didn't care if the food was good or bad, I just needed to eat something and go to bed. I had no idea how I'd even be able to sleep that night, but I knew I was physically and mentally tired. It was always good in theory to go and get a good night's sleep, but when's the last time anybody had a "good night's sleep" anyway? I mean…I was always tired.

Usually, as soon as my head would hit the pillow, that one little thought would creep inside my mind. Not a big thought, just a little itch, an itch that wasn't debilitating at first, yet it couldn't be ignored. If it's scratched, then it becomes a bump, then a sore, then a rash and a complete breakout all over my body. Once I have a breakout, then I know I'm not going to sleep for a couple of hours. I could watch TV, read a book, do some dishes and it won't matter, those are all temporary distractions, just quick relief with no resolution to the problem. What school will my child get into next year? What if I lose my job? Can I afford this house? Why is my spouse behaving this way towards me? Even mundane issues like whether or not I'll be able to get my oil changed on the weekend could keep me awake. There is very little a person can do that will resolve the matter. I could write myself a note or something to make sure I didn't forget whatever task was keeping me up at night because I was scared I'd forget whatever it was that I needed to do. Yet I still would worry. The next day I would go about my business and forget to address the issue that disturbed me the night before in the first place. It was a sickening cycle. I would forget my worries during the day because I would be distracted, mostly involuntarily by the duties required of me. I created duties at night to avoid the issue that was worrying me and adhere to these duties during the day, which forced me to avoid the very issue at hand! I couldn't get any sleep and didn't want to deal with the issue because I'd be too tired.

What's the solution? The solution is a change in circumstances. One doesn't worry about oil changes and schools if the world is ending. If a person has terminal cancer, that person doesn't stay up at night wondering if the neighbor will ever stop letting their dog use the front lawn as a toilet. If someone is being chased from their village in the Sudan because their family was murdered during an ethnic cleansing, then that person doesn't worry about when one can make it to the grocery store or whether they'll make partner at the firm. Horror can liberate a mind from the trivial worries pushed upon oneself in the first world. A refugee child escaping civil war doesn't contemplate his purpose in life or his career choices or whether or not he'll truly "find himself", at least not at the moment, because he's already found himself…he's hungry, scared and tired. That is his identity … someone trying to keep from dying. His purpose is to survive, to eat, to avoid being killed and to protect his loved ones or reunite with them. Drop someone off in the desert and tell them to survive and they'll be instantly cured from whatever obsessive compulsive disorder, restless leg syndrome or need for "me time" that's causing them to "suffer".

While at no point would I consider the experience I was going through as the same as some sort of war experience or terminal disease, it was a certainly precarious. When I drove to the hotel, I drove in a fog. So when a driver honked and cursed at me for some self-created conflict on the road, I didn't give it a second thought. A slight on the roads had no bearing on my life at that moment in time. No, I wasn't facing imminent death, but it did feel like death wasn't particularly far off and there was a real danger coming my way. I didn't care how the food tasted. I just knew that I needed a bite before bed. I sat down for a meal and a chance to contemplate how my approach to Deputy Garza would be the next day.

The waitress dropped by with a menu and some sort of bourbon drink that I didn't order. I informed her so as I rarely drank anymore, especially by myself. She pointed across the restaurant and there was Mr. Carlisle, raising a glass to me. My heart sank as I was hoping to avoid this man. I was beginning to realize that he was smarter than me or at least knew much more information than I knew, which put him in a position of power and manipulation. I didn't know what his endgame was, but I was sure that my best interests were not in his mind, given that he'd put me in the terrible situation in the first place. Mr. Carlisle smiled and began to make his way over to me. He seemed a little more threatening to me at that moment, like he was a bit younger or snappier dresser. I couldn't quite put my finger on it other than he seemed to have a bit of glow about him…a menacing glow at that.

Without waiting for an invitation, Mr. Carlisle took a seat at my table. Still smiling, he looked me over for a moment, chuckled to himself and raised his glass to me a second time as if to give me a toast. For what, I couldn't imagine as it seemed the last time we met he was a bit frustrated with me.

Mr. Carlisle motioned to my unsolicited drink and asked, "It's rude to not drink good whiskey that a friend buys for you."

"Not much of a drinker," I retorted.

"That's right, you stuck to water last time. Do you not enjoy my company or do you think you're a better man than me?"

"Good question, I might be better than you in some areas I guess…I'm sure you're better than me in others."

"You didn't address whether you liked me or not…my feelings are hurt," said Mr. Carlisle, still smiling. His teeth were so bright, for a moment I thought they were made of gold, especially juxtaposed to the smoke suddenly swirling around his face. Apparently, he had decided that he was allowed to smoke cigars inside the restaurant. I'm not sure what decade he thought he was living in, but I couldn't imagine any restaurant in this day and age allowing him to smoke. Mr. Carlisle must have sensed my thoughts because he directly addressed the issue, "You don't think I can smoke in here? Let me tell you something junior…I can do whatever the hell I want!" This was a bit aggressive for Mr. Carlisle. Usually he just came off as snarky or arrogant. This proclamation sounded like it came from an aggressive drunk.

Mr. Carlisle looked into my eyes, lingering without blinking. He nodded up at the waitress who stopped by the table and proceeded to ask Mr. Carlisle to put out his cigar. She was polite and did so in a hushed voice as to mistakenly allow her patron to not be embarrassed. However, Mr. Carlisle was not the sort to believe in embarrassment when it came to his own brash behavior.

"Or what?" Mr. Carlisle retorted.

"I…I guess I'll have to get the manager," the nervous waitress replied.

"And then what?" asked Mr. Carlisle.

"I'm sure he'll call the police if you don't…put out the..," the waitress responded, now looking around and hoping for some help. Nobody was paying attention.

"Why don't you just cut out the middle man and call the police? Here's why… whatever authority you think your manager has will certainly not be enough to persuade me to put out my damn cigar. So why don't you call the police and avoid the whole charade," advised Mr. Carlisle. At this point, I'd gone beyond uncomfortable and became angry at how he was treating the waitress. Her face was reddening and she was staring at her shoes…like as if she were a kindergartner. It was a terrible scene to witness. She had gone from being a perky server, whose goal was to make our dinner enjoyable…to serve us, which is a noble pursuit, to now being reduced to nothing and for no reason other than a man wanting to smoke a cigar and not adhere to the rules. I don't care the price of that cigar, it could not have been more valuable than this woman's self-worth. But to him…it was fun. She was a ball of yarn to bat around a bit until something more entertaining came along.

I decided to intervene, "Just put out the cigar out and leave the lady alone." I turned to the waitress to apologize.

"Why are you apologizing? She's a grown-up, she can handle herself. Do you think she's stupid? Ma'am, my friend here thinks you're stupid. Do you think you're stupid?" Mr. Carlisle asked the waitress. She shook her head from side to side in response. By now, she wasn't talking. She still did not look up from the ground, but she was listening

"Leave her alone and put out the damn cigar!" I demanded.

"My friend here is patronizing you. He doesn't think much of you. You see, he thinks you're so bad at your job, that you can't get a little nonthreatening guy like myself to put out a cigar. Actually, it's much worse. You see, he thinks you're so low, that you don't even have the brain capacity to speak for yourself. Isn't that insulting? Don't guys like him make you mad, always intervening on behalf of you like you're some kind of helpless infant? Sweetheart, let me ask you something, why do you want me to put out the cigar so bad? Are you such a child that you can't handle a little cigar smoke?" asked Mr. Carlisle.

"It's…it's not that. I'll get in trouble if I let you smoke here," the waitress responded, her face still flush with embarrassment.

"You could get fired too," said Mr. Carlisle. The waitress shook her head up and down in response. Mr. Carlisle smiled and continued, "Tell you what, I'll give you a hundred bucks if you let me smoke in here. If your manager comes by and says something about it, I'll put my cigar out and say that I had just lit it up and you didn't know about it, so you won't get in trouble. Sound good?" The waitress smiled and nodded with approval. Mr. Carlisle pulled out a hundred dollars and stuffed it in the waitress' pocket. She turned to leave and Mr. Carlisle caught her and asked, "Who's your favorite, me or him?" Without hesitation, the waitress pointed to Mr. Carlisle.

"See…I can do anything I want," he smiled and patted himself on the belly as if he'd just had a big meal. In some ways he did have a meal as he'd devoured two egos swiftly, gorging on our carcasses without much of a thought to it.

"I guess you can do what you want, in an extremely roundabout way," I said. I was not impressed by his behavior.

"Doesn't matter, I got where I needed to go. It doesn't matter how you get there," Mr. Carlisle responded.

"To you I guess, but to me you should adhere to some semblance of a moral code," I responded.

Mr. Carlisle looked taken aback, "Really? Have you turned yourself in for your attempted bribery of a judge? No? Strange, by now you're at least an accessory by not going to

66

the cops. You've had the knowledge for a while now. Most people would have gone to the authorities much sooner than you." Mr. Carlisle chuckled, looked down at his drink and said, "Don't worry though, I'm with you on this one. Keep it to yourself so you can handle everything. Why bring in the bumbling cops? You and I are in this together."

"Nope. I'm not in anything with you. You're the one that got me into all this. I'd love to never see you again. I'm not sure why you're here in the first place," I said.

"Why don't you like me? Are you religious or something?" Mr. Carlisle circled back to discuss this issue.

I hesitated. Nobody really asked me that before. Of course I was religious, I went to church almost every other week. It was strange that it took this long for someone to ask me if I was religious. I guess nobody really cared or maybe they just never suspected I was a man of God. Maybe it didn't show.

"Yes, I am religious," I responded. It sounded so odd coming from my own mouth. It didn't feel comfortable, which didn't make sense. If I went to church and didn't hide that fact, why would I feel uncomfortable telling someone at dinner that I was religious?

"Good. I'm sure you're very versed in the good book, right?" Mr. Carlisle asked tauntingly. I nodded in agreement, although I wasn't particularly confident in where this was leading or in my own knowledge of my own beliefs, if I were to be honest.

"So that's why you don't like me? You're religious, so you want to disassociate with your bribery scandal and drinking with an old acquaintance, right?" asked Mr. Carlisle.

"Yeah…something like that I guess," I responded, still trying to understand where he was going with this topic.

"That's interesting. You actually think you're better than me just because you're more religious than me. I find that hard to believe. You go to a building once a week or every other week and sing a song, so that makes you better than me? Well I'm versed in the Bible myself...I guess you find that hard to believe? Let me ask you something, have you ever unintentionally sinned?" asked Mr. Carlisle.

"Of course, everybody has at some point unintentionally sinned. It happens on a daily basis," I responded.

"Well...what did you do about it?"

"If I realized that I unintentionally sinned, I repented and tried to do better next time."

"So you disobeyed God?"

"No! How did you get that out of what I said?" I responded a bit angrily. I was getting annoyed by Mr. Carlisle's little exercise.

"I guess I'm a little more informed than you. The way I understand it, once you realize your guilt *and* the sin you commit becomes known, then you must bring a female goat, without defect mind you, lay your hands on the goat's head and slaughter it at a place where you give a burnt offering. Have you done that yet? No? Really? Well, it doesn't end there. Then the priest has to take some of the goat's blood, remember I'm talking about a female goat without defect whom you've slaughtered...the priest takes the goat's blood with his finger and puts it on the horns of the altar of burnt offering and pours out the rest of the blood at the base of the altar. Did the priest do that for you yet? No? Wow, not particularly religious are we? Wait, I'm not finished. You've now got to remove the fat, you know...just like you do with a fellowship offering, and the priest shall, not may, but *shall* burn the fat. You understand that you must burn the fat! Of course you probably already know that this is an aroma pleasing to the Lord. Your

68

Lord! Have you done that every time you've committed an unintentional sin?"[39] Mr. Carlisle paused, his smile was sickening to me. He must have scoured the text to find some passage to trick me. For what? What did he care about my biblical knowledge?

I didn't dignify his snarky little game with a response, though my lack of acknowledgement did not seem to bother him. Mr. Carlisle took another sip from his drink, this time exaggerating his pleasure with a loud gasp at the end of his swallow. He even looked at his glass admiringly as if he was drinking the most exquisite drink available.

He continued his mockery of my beliefs, "Let's try a different dilemma? What if instead of a goat, you bring a lamb to atone for your sins? We've all been there right? It seems certain, given your lack of religious knowledge that you wouldn't know this, but I'll help you out as I assume you aren't well read on the subject. If you decide to go with a lamb instead of a goat, once again you need to go with a female with no defect, don't forget no defect, then you do all the stuff you would do to a goat, only with a lamb.[40] Not complicated, but still in need of being addressed I think you'll agree. You see, sometimes we have goats around, sometimes we have lambs. I think it's reasonable for your god to give you the choice of convenience here…goat or lamb. He must love you very much. So, I'm assuming you have been slaughtering lots of goats or lambs lately haven't you?"

Once again, I didn't respond. For one, I didn't know how to respond, for it was clear that he either knew something I did not or he was just making stuff up as he went along. Either way, it would be a pointless battle. It didn't seem to matter as Mr. Carlisle clearly wanted to continue with his ridicule, probably more for his own amusement than anything.

---

[39] Lev. 4:27-31
[40] Lev. 4:32-35

"Let's talk women shall we? You ever touch your wife during her period? I'll repeat it louder in case you didn't hear me, have…you…touched…your…wife when she's on her period?" I didn't respond. Mr. Carlisle continued, "I'll assume yes. I mean none of us want to be around a woman on her period, but you being a sensitive guy, I'm sure you've given your wife a good pat on the back or a hug or even touched her bed or chair during her time of the month right? I guess it's safe to assume you've done your duty and ran off and cleaned yourself and your clothes for the evening correct? I mean, you'd be unclean as well, so you'll need to separate from everyone else until the evening. You knew that right?[41] If you haven't been doing so, it's an affront to your god and he loves you and wants you to follow the rules right?"

"What's your point? That I'm not religious because I don't follow some outdated obscure passages from the Bible? That's suspect," I replied.

"It's Leviticus! Leviticus is outdated and obscure…really?"

"It's not the New Testament, so I guess so," I was getting shaky on my reasoning and he knew it.

"The New Testament is two thousand years old, I would say that's a bit outdated as well don't you think? I think we find ourselves on a bit of a slippery slope don't you think?" Mr. Carlisle asked with a chuckle. "You go to church right?" he continued.

"Every Sunday. The God of the New Testament is gentle and loving. There's not the need to get into legalism. Bringing in the rules of the Old Testament is old hats. It's the usual method religious critics use to show some sort of inconsistency or to ridicule some ancient laws about hygiene and so forth," I replied. I was growing more confident with my ability to out logic Mr. Carlisle.

---

[41] Lev. 15:19-33

"You give all your belongings to the church? Do you ever lie about how much you're going to give? Do you fill out one of those pledge cards and come up short at the end of the year? I'm sure you've got a million excuses. Remember Ananias and Sapphira? No? They're not mentioned much are they? Not a lot of artwork devoted to them is there? All sorts of scenes from your lovely book have been painted or sculpted, but not poor Ananias or Sapphira. You remember what they did right? Sold some property and gave a nice donation to the church. Sounds good right? But no, they had the good sense to save a small portion for a rainy day and your god...your so called loving god struck them both down dead, husband and wife...dead for saving a bit of money.[42] What a compassionate god you have there. Have you saved your money or have you given it all to the church, every last penny? Because if you didn't give everything, you should be dead. Are you dead? No? I guess that means there's no god...right? I guess it's possible that you gave all your belongings to the church, but I'm going to go out on a limb here and say you didn't. Yet there you sit before me...sinner...making a mockery of your god...a god that either doesn't adhere to his own rules or, or does not actually exist. It's one or the other isn't it? Why not forget all of this nonsense and focus on accomplishing an actual goal for once in your life? If you really don't want to die, you need to create a legacy, that's immortality right? That's how you become immortal. You get followers, money, a name on a company, a damn brick named after you on the new wing of the children's hospital! If there is a god, he knows that in the day you reach success, be it financial, artistic or philanthropic, your eyes will be opened and you will be like God, knowing good and evil at the same time and you will not die![43]" Mr. Carlisle smirked and watched me, very pleased with himself.

---

[42] Acts 5
[43] Gen. 3:4-5

I stared at this man, this man who just a couple of years past seemed nonthreatening, yet always unnerving. Now he appeared to be borderline evil. He evolved, or devolved if you will, from a one time irritant to someone who may quite frankly ruin my life, and he seemed to be enjoying himself. Who was this guy and why had he all of a sudden popped up into my life in such a significant manner recently? Was it chance that this man I'd met in the past also happened to have some sort of perverted interest in my pro bono work? Or was it that I just happened to be the poor sap assigned a matter that crossed paths with a man heavily involved in corruption? He was smarter than me, that fact was for sure. He didn't seem to have a conscious, which meant he would be more successful than me and more effective. A conscious slows a person down. Why was he tied to me?

"Where have you been?" I asked bluntly. Mr. Carlisle looked up from his drink suddenly. He seemed to be surprised by the question.

"What?" he asked.

"I said…where have you been? I met you once a couple of years ago at an elevator. I never saw you again until this matter came up. Where have you been?" I demanded.

"Me? Oh…I've been around. Hell, the partner that sent you on this worthless mission of mercy was with me at the jiggle joint not but a couple of weeks ago. We had quite a night! It was not suitable for younger viewers if you can imagine, but you probably couldn't imagine, knowing you. People might see you at such a place and your gold façade would be tarnished. But that guy! Man, skin for skin[44] is what he's all about," replied Mr. Carlisle.

"He never mentioned you," I said.

---

[44] Job 2:4

"That guy? He barely knows my name. You know, some of us can creep along unnoticed, even if we're designated for condemnation.[45] Besides, he blacks out. He's got an instant excuse for his behavior because he doesn't remember it. So, he either says he didn't do anything wrong or he apologizes and says he doesn't remember. It's a great system! He's profane, I guess I'm a profane thing as well[46]," Mr. Carlisle said.

"Yeah, but where have you been, physically? Were you just lingering around the office waiting for this little project or were you waiting for me? Am I some sort of entertainment for you or I am just naïve enough for you to use me unknowingly in some sort of scheme?" I asked.

"Oh I'm sure it's a little bit from all of the above. You were pretty self-absorbed your first couple of years at the firm, so I'm guessing you just didn't notice me so much. I've been there though…been there a long time. I guess you could say I'm the prince of the power of the air[47]," Mr. Carlisle explained.

I was physically tired and by now was mentally tired of Mr. Carlisle's little games. It was time to get to the point, "So what do you want?"

He sat back in his chair, took another long obnoxious drink, gasped again and began, "I'm here to talk about the money. It's gone, correct?" I nodded. "Well…that's a big, big problem son. I'm just a facilitator, you understand? I really don't do anything personally; I just help make things happen. It's like a river, I just help keep the water flowing. If someone resists me, then I flee from them.[48] I am far enough removed to not be privy to the exact identity of the payer, I just know the identity of the payee. I don't personally interact with either. I'm a man who knows a man who knows another man. This gives me a sliver of all things, but keeps me

---

[45] Jude 1:4
[46] Eze 28:16
[47] Eph. 2:2
[48] James 4:7

from any real danger. I don't know who the man with the money is, but I know he's probably really bad; bad enough to do nasty things to you and those around you. I'm here to remind you that in spite of our little argument back there, you are an extremely intelligent guy. You are a capable person. That's why you were chosen for such tasks down here. The Rio Grande Valley is a complicated spot. It seems simple, but it's not. Right and wrong are often subjective. When you're at a border, you're in a world of hardship and temptation all rolled up into a tangled mess of confusion. It's all a bunch of grey areas, very little black and white. Everyone's friendly and everyone's capable of questionable decisions. The border is just that, a border…a border that rides the edge of right and wrong. But you…you are unshakable. You can handle this. Yes, you made a bad decision. All you had to do was drop something off and you screwed it up. Now a really bad enterprise is out of its investment and people that work together in an already precarious fashion are walking around with one finger on the trigger. Things are likely to blow-up in a manner that you can't possibly imagine. However, you can mitigate things. You can't stop the bad, but you can keep the bad from becoming worse. I'm telling you that it will be best for you and all those around you if you just handle this yourself. You go to the authorities and the Rio Grande will turn red with blood, more blood than you've ever seen, son. You handle this yourself. Depend on your own understanding, you're smart. I'm off."

I felt like I had heard the opposite before, do not depend on your own understanding.[49] Didn't someone say that to me before? I couldn't remember. Was Mr. Carlisle right or my own shrouded memory? He was out the door without a glance back in my direction. He was gone.

---

[49] Prov. 3:5

Mr. Carlisle was compelling, but I wanted more information. I didn't trust him of course, but I didn't trust myself either. I would find Deputy Garza. I needed more information, and he was the next step in the process.

Chapter 7 – The Deputy.

I awoke the next day with little memory of going to bed. I had nothing to drink, no medicine, just the natural hallucinogen of stress and sleep deprivation to create a fog of the night before. I remember Mr. Carlisle and our conversation, but anything beyond Mr. Carlisle's departure was a blur. It was just a series of images. My face in the mirror becoming distorted with the florescent lighting and dark background, the dark circles under my eyes looking like bruises, turning off a lamp and blackness. The lamp…a smoking oven and a flaming torch passing between pieces.[50] I had to make my lamps seven in number, why? To shed light on the space in front of them?[51] The pure candlestick…with the lamps thereof…even with the lamps to be set in order, and…all the vessels thereof. [52] These were the thoughts clouding my mind, lamps, candlesticks, lights…for the first time in my life, nothing in my head was making sense. At this point I was sitting outside my body, outside my mind…my body just functioning without thought, my mind thinking of lamps and torches for reasons I could not decipher. My mind just went into these things, in a whirlwind, in a panic like I had to figure it out at that moment before being engulfed.

I needed to dress and find Deputy Garza. I was compelled to have answers. I was being pushed by outside forces or internal. I didn't think much of Mr. Carlisle's advice or persuasion, although I had no way of knowing if what he had said sank into my consciousness. I knew he wanted me to handle the matter myself, which is what I was doing, but I was also planning on meeting with a deputy of the sheriff's department, so I guess I was technically going to an authority for help as well. But I wasn't seeking help, I was seeking answers and I had no way of

---

[50] Gen. 15:17
[51] Exod. 25:37
[52] Exod. 39:37

knowing where on the moral line Garza stood. If he was a willing participant to this corruption, he could easily dispatch of me and nobody would know. Worse than that, he could openly get rid of me and have some sort of misdeed pinned to me as an alibi. When government or law enforcement goes bad, there's very little a citizen can do in the short term to protect themselves other than not getting involved in the first place. Most unfortunate for me, I was involved regardless of my intentions. I was stuck and I was a target. If I were to successfully contact Garza, my fate would be in his hands.

I checked the appraisal district's website to see if I could find out where Deputy Garza lived. I wasn't shocked to find a massive amount of people with the last name of "Garza" to be homeowners in the area. Even after filtering the list down to "R", "Rudy" or "Rudolpho" as first names didn't narrow the field down far enough to pay a visit. However, after a bit of social media searching and other web postings, I was able to find one address that seemed to match. I decided then was as good a time as any to visit Rudy Garza, so I headed out and hoped for the best.

Garza's house was small, but neat and well maintained. The neighborhood looked like any other lower middle class residential area, basically family homes from what I could determine. If a vehicle was in view, it was a truck for sure. That was standard fair in Texas, especially in the Valley. Sure enough, a big, shiny pick-up was sitting there in Garza's driveway. I had no doubt it was his. Most people around here had a higher monthly payment on their truck than their house.

With a breath, I parked and approached the house and knocked. That moment was going to determine the course of my existence. After a pause, the door opened and Deputy Rudy Garza stood before me. He looked me up and down suspiciously in silence. I waited for him to say something, but he did not.

Nervously, I cleared my throat and took a step forward, as if I were some old timey door to door salesman, "Deputy Garza?"

He continued to look intensely upon me, as if measuring me for something, maybe sizing me up.

"Who's asking?"

"My name is Martin Dye, I'm an attorney," I was quickly cut off as Garza began to shut the door.

"I've got union representation, goodbye," said Garza abruptly.

"Wait! It's not about that…it's about someone who died on the river. I was sent here to represent him…he was burned!" I shouted. Garza paused and looked at me for a moment as his face softened with concern.

"Which one?" he asked. I was confused. Who else could it be?

"What do you mean? The boy…from Honduras, who else could it be?" I had never heard that there were others.

"Oh…they are gradually passing away. It hasn't made it to the news. Not much really does that they don't want you to know about," Rudy said with a smirk. He continued, "My guess is that a few more people will disappear. That's how things go when something like this happens," he paused, took a breath and continued, "My grandpa always told me about this red horse. He'd have a little campfire going late at night and I'd come and sit on the dirt across from him and after a few shots of something he'd ramble on about the old times, which meant stories of dead friends and relatives. Grandad would sort of drift off, looking at the fire, he looked possessed, and he'd say '…and there was this horse that would come out of the wilderness, a red horse, and whenever it showed up it would take peace from the land and people would put one another to death…'[53] I had no idea what he was talking about, but whenever something like this happens…in the back of my mind I think this red horse has come back out and caused everyone to kill each other. That's the only way I can make sense of something like this."

"Something like this? Has this happened before?" I asked a bit surprised.

Rudy Garza paused for a bit, then answered, "Things happen all the time. This…this was a bit different. They seem to be getting worse, but stuff happens and people disappear. The red horse."

"Will that game warden disappear? Robin Keller?" I asked. Rudy Garza's eyes darted at me with a nervous energy and he opened the door and motioned for me to come inside. It was clear that he was concerned about Robin, but why? Was he out to get rid of her or was he genuinely concerned about her well-being?

His house was modest, but clean and organized. Framed picture of his family were all over the place. It was easy to determine that he was married and had at least two kids. He appeared to be alone for the time being. Rudy noticed that I was looking at the pictures and briefly explained that his wife was at work, she was a nurse, and his sons were in school. He said he keeps in shape, but was on paid leave, so he was making the best of the situation. I asked why he was on leave, but I received no response. It was apparent that for now at least, Rudy Garza would be asking the questions.

"When did you talk to the game warden?" he asked.

"Just a day or so ago, why? What do you know?"

---

[53] Rev. 6:4

"No, that's not how it's going to be. What do *you* know?" Deputy Garza nodded over to a gun he had sitting on the table, to make sure I understood him.

"I know that I was sent here to represent the boy who was burned in the crossing fire. This was supposed to be a charitable representation, immigration status, medical care, and so forth, but he died."

"Did you speak with him?" Rudy asked. I wasn't sure how I should answer this as I didn't know if it would be better to say yes or no. I was never a good liar and my guess was that the less information known the better, so I shook my head "no".

"Then why are you still here? You should be back home right? He's dead," said Rudy.

"Well, I was hoping to help the others. However, I'm a bit disturbed that they are beginning to die off. As you say…these things happen, but are they supposed to happen? I wanted to talk to the Game Warden because she witnessed the whole mess. I thought she might give me some insight. She just so happened to mention that you'd been trying to contact her, so I thought I would speak to you and figure out not only what's going on, but how I could help the remaining victims," I said. Now, I was lying. I should have been helping the others, but my motivation was not to help others, but to save myself and my family. In the eyes of some that would be a noble enough cause, but I knew better. I was saving my own hide. My hope was that Garza wouldn't see how poor of a liar I was and would help me out with some information.

The deputy looked me over for a bit, glanced towards some of the pictures on the wall and sighed, resolved to some sort of inevitable fate. He shook his head to himself looking down at his legs, as if he were alone, then looked back up at me with solemn eyes.

"Something wasn't right. At first there was no real probable cause to pull the guy over, but I knew I'd recognized him before. The driver. The time of day to be transporting was a little off. The whole thing was strange. My senior deputy was acting different too. And then I found out about the river and was suspended. That's why I tried to call the Game Warden. I wanted to know what she saw. People said it was unrelated, but it couldn't be, the timing was just too big of a deal," Rudy paused again, looking up at the ceiling now, like he was trying to gather himself. He must have felt the same way I did with Robin, a need to not be alone in this situation. There were very few people to trust, I'm sure he wanted to tell someone what he knew. We would end up spending about an hour together, discussing what happened, through the course of our conversation, I began to understand the man a little better.

Deputy Rudolfo "Rudy" Garza had been a part of the sheriff's department for a couple of years by then. He'd become acclimated to his job, but there were times when he wished that he had a bit more experience, especially concerning all the different law enforcement organizations involved in the valley. I guess you could say that Rudy, until recently, was naïve in perception of all the law enforcement agencies, in thinking that everyone should work together to serve in the best interest of justice. It was a bit strange, given that he grew up in this area; an area where corruption and self-serving government entities were not uncommon. If I were to have believed Rudy, it would seem that he was not in on the joke and that he was a bit on the outside. Rudy described it like there was a club and he was never asked to join. Everyone in the sheriff's department apparently liked him, he said he was social and never really had any major dust-ups with anyone. He was often invited to go out after work, though he usually declined because he had a wife and kids and felt he needed to be home most of the time. He told me that he just had some sort of vibe that he wasn't part of the group. It was likely a separation by choice to an extent. He could have chosen to enjoy passing pleasures rather than endure ill-treatment, but he was considering greater treasure.[54]

Rudy told me about a drug bust that took place over a year ago during his first year as deputy. It was a huge marijuana bust, which was being transported in the back of a home renovation van associated with an actual local home renovation company. Rudy wasn't exactly sure how or why the bust occurred, but within a day or so, there were city detectives, the sheriff's department, a Texas Ranger, Border Patrol, National Guard, the DEA, Secret Service, FBI and even a private security company all getting involved.

That's how it was, if something of note crosses the border illegally, a whole lot of entities get involved in some form. Rudy had recalled to a DEA agent that he and the Sheriff had pulled over that same van in the past. It turned out that after the Sheriff ran the plates and spoke to the driver, there was a misunderstanding and they let them go with a warning. Rudy never thought much of the incident other than the fact that the driver was missing his left earlobe. A person just doesn't see that every day. Once word got back to the office that Rudy had divulged this information, the senior deputy Gus Bauer spoke to Rudy about it and let him know that Rudy should have cleared things with him first. Rudy was confused, but agreed. He just wanted to follow protocol and do the best job he could do. The Sheriff never seemed mad, but Rudy was always disappointed that he'd made such a mistake and he felt like he just wasn't involved in the conversation.

During most of his second year on the job, Rudy shadowed Gus Bauer on patrols and assignments. He got along great with Gus. Even after Gus reprimanded him a bit for talking to the DEA agent, they worked well together. Gus liked Rudy's drive and constant strive to get better as a peace officer. Gus especially appreciated the fact that Rudy was so coachable. If Gus needed to correct Rudy on a procedure, all he had to do was tell Rudy once and it was corrected,

[54] Heb. 11:25-26

which was a rare occurrence in the first place. Rudy never questioned the reasoning behind Gus' methods, he just assumed that a more experienced officer knew better.

Deputy Garza had given me this massive background…me, a complete stranger. It was odd. I might have been the only person he could talk to about it. He certainly couldn't complain to his superiors of such things and I'm guessing he didn't want his wife knowing any troubles as well. Maybe he was seeking such companionship with Robin. Who knows?

Rudy took a breath and then began to tell me about his day, the day when the boy and the others were burned. That particular morning was no different to Rudy than any other he said to me. He was driving on patrol with Gus Bauer sitting next him, talking about what they needed to do that day and what shows they watched the night before. Gus was still the guy with which Rudy needed to clear everything and was always around him as they were assigned to each other. Per usual, they were to stop over at a particular coffee shop to get a couple of to-go coffees and get the day started. They also intended to stop by their favorite tamale stand for breakfast.

I found it strange to eat tamales in the morning, but Rudy insisted that it was common practice especially for the ones with cream cheese and jalapeno. He said they were delicious and that Gus loved them and never started a day without at least one. That particular day, Gus refused, which was absolutely bizarre to Rudy. He likened Gus without a breakfast tamale to a dog using a litter box, it just didn't make sense for this change in behavior all of a sudden and probably meant something was wrong. Rudy noticed that Gus seemed a little off as the morning had progressed. Normally Gus was pretty boisterous and chipper, on this particular day he seemed run down and didn't seem to want to talk. Rudy also noticed that Gus had his shirt pulled in tight, as if he was cold.

Rudy asked Gus if he was okay and Gus just nodded. They made it to the coffee shop, Rudy hopped out and waited for Gus, who seemed to struggle just to get out of the car. Rudy made the determination that Gus was clearly sick and needed to go home, especially if he were going to be interacting with Rudy and other officers. The department didn't like sickness heroes either. One man with the flu can cripple the place in a week. However, Gus insisted that he was fine.

Rudy went ahead and ordered the coffees and waited for Gus, who slowly trudged into the shop and plopped down on a chair. Gus was an okay deputy and all, but Rudy told me that he'd never witnessed the guy power through an illness to be at work. Gus wasn't that type of officer. Rudy put the coffees in the car and again waited for Gus. Finally, Gus made it, strapped himself in and rested his head against the window. For most of the day, Rudy kept trying to make small talk, making sure that Gus wasn't in serious jeopardy. Gus would nod, respond tersely, and then go back to leaning against the window.

By the afternoon, Rudy had grown tired of the whole business. Rudy had finally blown up and told Gus that he was pretty useless and that all he was really accomplishing was potentially making Rudy sick. Rudy insisted that Gus go home, rest up and that they'd catch up sometime later that week. Gus wouldn't have anything to do with it.

At this point, Rudy had determined that Gus was a liability and potentially a danger to others if they need to get him to the hospital. He decided to radio the Sheriff to get Gus to go home. Gus shook his head no, but Rudy ignored him. Rudy went back and forth with the Sheriff, who seemed unconcerned with the situation and ultimately decided to let Gus make the call as to whether he needed to go home or not. Rudy was shocked, as he thought surely the Sheriff would have made Gus go home, especially in his current condition.

Rudy handed the radio to Gus, who suddenly perked up and told the Sheriff that he was good to go. Just like that, the matter was resolved. Then Rudy felt like something else was going on, once again behind his back. He couldn't imagine Gus fighting through sickness to be there. Rudy stared at Gus with a questionable look, but Gus turned away and leaned on the window again. While Rudy thought the whole thing was odd, he was done with it as well. Once the decision was made, Rudy was ready to go about his duties, regardless of Gus' capacity.

The afternoon moved along without much of an incident, a ticket here and there and one call regarding some stolen merchandise, nothing strange other than the fact the Gus basically slept most of the time with a fever. Rudy drove him around, stopping occasionally to pick up some Tylenol to knock down the fever a bit. The afternoon was finally winding down for the men, a fresh pair of legs was going to take their place, but Gus insisted they take their time as he just wasn't feeling good enough to be in a hurry. Rudy was ready to head home for some dinner, especially after dealing with Gus all day. They had stopped to gas up and Gus wanted to sit on the bench in front of the gas station for a bit before they were done.

Rudy was about to protest until something else caught his attention. It was an old beat up suburban pulling up to the stop sign next to the gas station, just to the right of Rudy. The windows were heavily tinted and it was being driven a bit slower than normal. He couldn't put his finger on it, but something about it didn't seem right. Rudy had told me that when you're in law enforcement, you look for things abnormal. You profile. The suburban was just not driving like a normal car.

Then he noticed the driver…missing that left earlobe.

Rudy yelled at Gus to get moving, he was ready to follow this guy. When Gus looked at Rudy and saw that Rudy was ready to pursue, Gus seemed to be reluctant, almost nervous. Rudy said that Gus was fervently trying to convince him not to follow the vehicle, that there was

nothing to gain. This only intrigued Rudy further because in Rudy's mind, if there was no issue,

then what's the problem? Why not follow the guy? Besides, how many men in the area were

missing the exact same earlobe of a driver that was busted and let go in the past? At that point in

time, Rudy had decided that he would follow this man, and he couldn't care less what Gus

thought about it. Rudy's instincts as a law officer had kicked in and his desire to protect, which

he was born with, also took precedent over any reservations he might have had up to that point.

As Rudy put it, Gus mustered a renewed energy to jump into the car with Rudy to pursue

the suburban. However, it was clear that Gus was not motivated to confront or even follow this

individual, he was more intent on trying to convince Rudy not to proceed. Gus kept telling Rudy

to wait, but wait for what?

While the driver was not technically doing anything wrong, because Rudy recognized the

driver as a suspected drug runner, he was becoming increasingly tense and focused in on the

potential dangers of the pursuit. They slowly followed the suburban; Rudy was not hiding the

fact that he was following the guy as he was in a sheriff's car and there was no way they could

have sneaked up on him. Rudy wanted probable cause to search and he was intent on following

the suspect all night if needed. It became clear to Rudy that the driver knew the game as he

began to change speeds rapidly, just to signal to Rudy that he was aware. Rudy stayed close

behind. Gus continued to try and convince him to forget about the whole thing.

The slow chase was in the middle of a crowded area of town, so Rudy was willing to bide

his time as he was concerned about the civilians. The driver was cognizant of this fact, and used

it to his advantage. A school bus, full of extended daycare kids pulled up at a stop a few blocks

down and Rudy's spirits dropped at the sight of it. He explained to me that when a drug runner knows he's being followed, they will often follow close to a school bus, knowing that law enforcement won't make a move when they're that close to kids. Such a tactic wasn't necessarily successful, but it was used in times of desperation, just to add another dangerous element to the mix. Drug runners didn't have a lot of leverage against law enforcement, but one aspect that was always in their favor was their lack of respect for human life and what was more precious than the lives of children?

Rudy pulled out and tried to speed around to cut off the driver before he got to the bus, but the driver was already on his way and was within a few feet of the back of it. Rudy could see some of the kids watching from the rear, unaware of the potential danger in play. The suspect slowly crept along behind the bus, stopping and waiting at every stop as each kid descended the steps and ran home for the evening. Each time a kid jumped off the bus, the suspect would look back at Rudy in his side mirror to make sure Rudy could see his smirk. He was just waiting and biding his time. At some point, the suspect would make a break, but when and how many lives would be in jeopardy?

This cat and mouse, start and stop slow chase went on for several blocks until they came upon a bridge. The bridge would be the spot and both men knew it. There were no stops on the bridge and beyond it were a few blocks of commercial land. The bridge was going to be the moment of reckoning. This was the spot where Rudy would try and overtake the suburban.

Rudy looked at me in such an intense manner that it felt as if we both were in the car together, white knuckled and ready to hit the gas, not knowing if we would make it out unscathed. He said that at that very moment, when he was ready to make the move, his radio came alive with a call for everyone to come to the river. Multiple victims, fire, illegal immigrants…just a mess. All officers were to help out. They never had all officers do anything all at once, it's just not safe, but that was the call.

Rudy wiped his brow a bit and was staring at the wall, I guess reliving the whole matter was intense. I never got too intense myself, so I couldn't really relate. Of course, I never was part of a car chase or any sort of criminal take down, so what do I know? Rudy snapped out of his daydream and went on to describe how agitated Gus became at that moment, screaming at Rudy to go to the river per the radio call, to forget about the suburban, but Rudy couldn't do it. There were kids, this guy was in the middle of the city, he needed to catch him, so he blocked out Gus' screaming as well as the radio and floored it.

The suburban sped up and shot around the school bus, then suddenly jolted to the right in an attempt to knock the bus off and cause more chaos. Rudy anticipated such an act of desperation and kept the pedal down to spin the suburban forward and away from the bus. The school bus driver slammed on the breaks with kids screaming and Rudy continue to push through the suburban, while calling for back up. The suburban hit the side rail and came to a stop. The driver, the man missing the ear lobe, hopped out and took off running down below the underpass. With no back up and Gus unwilling to help, Rudy decided to stay with the suburban and the school bus. The suspect was long gone.

"It was a massive bust, I'm talking cocaine here, real money," said Deputy Rudy Garza with a fleeting cadence of pride. He looked down, shook his head and continued, "After a long while, the Sheriff and another deputy showed up. The Sheriff looked sick. Here I thought I had the bust of the decade and Sheriff looked terrified. He didn't look angry or yell at me or anything, just looked scared and told me to go home. I haven't been back to work since."

I probed for answers regarding what happened to the drugs, but Rudy knew nothing and more or less stated that he was unwilling to personally look into the matter for obvious reasons. He has a nice family, this is the best career he could have as far as pay and benefits are concerned and at this point in time, he has plausible deniability of any shady dealings. By now I could tell that he did not want information from me, he didn't care to get to the bottom of this, he wanted to give me information. Rudy wanted to use me to protect other innocent witnesses, like Robin. He tried to reach out to her on his own, but failed as she wouldn't return his call, but now it was different. It's funny how people's minds work when given paid leave for a few days. He had time to think… to think about those closest to him, his future and so forth. He was moral, so he couldn't let it go, but he knew he was safe if he kept his mouth shut and probed no more. He knew the rules now. Rudy knew what to know and what not to know. Whether it be a sheriff's department or local police or anything for that matter, if corruption seeps in, an office needs a Boy Scout like Rudy to make it legitimate, but that Boy Scout needs to know the rules. Now Rudy knew, and he was not a whistleblower. The department must have sensed it or were giving him a chance to show he's no snitch otherwise he would be missing by now. They wouldn't have waited so long.

Rudy said what he had to say and that's all he would say. I took another chance and asked him if the same people ran the drugs and the illegals that day. Rudy wouldn't give me an answer other than, "It's a hell of a coincidence…but if it's not a coincidence…this was real bold, real cold. It can only get worse. I will tell you this, I'm guessing word got up to someone else about the drugs, not just the locals." With that, he led me out and shut the door.

As I walked away, the door opened again and Rudy stood there looking at me for a moment, then with solemn eyes said, "You know what they say…they come to you in sheep's clothing, but inwardly they are ferocious wolves.[55]" I turned and walked away without looking back.

Sometimes you'd like to go through a period of your life not knowing. Rudy chose that route, but forced me to gain knowledge, the kind of knowledge that I didn't want, but now had and I needed to deal with it. The heart of the discerning acquires knowledge, for the ears of the wise seek it out.[56] So, what happened? Was I bribing a judge and district attorney not to bring charges for the drug bust? What about the illegals, was I supposed to bribe them to look away from that too? Rudy said the guy got away, so who would they be bringing charges against? Had to be the suburban right? But why would some cartel have a car that could be traced? That didn't make any sense. Maybe it was just hush money in general. Rudy said word got out about the drugs. Could the feds be looking into it and the Judge and District Attorney be just two of many people being paid hush money.

Evil will never leave the house of one who pays back evil for good.[57] Maybe the guy with the missing earlobe got picked up by someone else. Maybe city police. Maybe he needed to be protected. I was in a bad spot. A cartel willing to set illegals on fire to get drugs across the border and the Sheriff being in on it. It was a distraction. They were willing to burn people alive just for the chance at distraction. It wasn't even a guarantee! A kid died just to give a drug runner a better chance. They wanted the immigrants to be noticed, to be watched crossing, so they didn't go at night. They wanted a distraction, a massive distraction for a massive drug move. I physically shivered when a new thought popped into my head. They burned people for

---

[55] Matt 7:15
[56] Prov. 18:15
[57] Prov. 17:13

a distraction, but if that cocaine is missing or in the hands of the DEA, police or anyone else for that matter…the bodies will be piling up. I assumed mine as well.

Chapter 8 – The Ranger.

By now, days, nights and hours were running together. I wasn't sure how long I'd been down there. I would check back on the calendar and realize it'd actually not been that long, but then forget and convince myself I'd been there for a month or two. The threat of violence and my family's life being ruined prevented much sleep other than involuntarily nodding off and the waking hours were filled mostly with a combination of dread, tight breathing and a head that felt as if it were expanding from the inside out. My skin had, or I perceived that it had, a greasy film covering it, as if I hadn't showered in a while, although I'm not sure if this was true.

I had a good life insurance policy, I mean good for my wife and kids. If I die, they get a couple million. If they die, we get a few thousand. The insurance company did not believe that my wife and kids were as valuable as me. Why? Because they don't earn anything. My wife actually went back to work recently, she told me so over the phone...she texted me. Not full time, but it's something, but not because it doesn't count as much as she actually earns according to the underwriter. The kids are valued about as much as the burial expenses, meaning they are not valued at all. More like loss of a pet if that pet had an expensive funeral. The world valued my family by how expensive they are and how much money they earned. I can't criticize that value system because it has become the norm anyway. How else would you quantify the loss? People either set their minds on things above or on earthly things.[58] I am valued infinitely higher, yet I have potentially caused infinite pain and suffering for my family if I am not able to pull out of this mess. I don't even really know if I'm in danger, it's speculation... educated speculation though. What is my value?

---

[58] Col. 3:2

The tighter the matter got around my neck, the more it was clear that I needed help. However, the deeper knowledge I obtained about the situation, the more I preferred not to go to the authorities. The more isolated I felt, the less clearly I began to think. Thus, the cause of my thoughts regarding my life insurance policy. Was it up to date? I couldn't have my wife marrying some scumbag child abuser in order to have financial support. It's a tough choice I assumed, marrying a piece of garbage or being broke right? If I checked on the insurance policy, what if I missed a payment? If I checked on the insurance policy, would that trigger suspicion? Would it? Yes it would, because I'd seen enough of those prime time who done it real life crime shows on television to know that if you check on your insurance right before you die, there is a presumption of foul play. Which is fine if I don't kill myself, but if I kill myself, what would the policy say? Would my family get the money if I committed the ultimate sin? If I just get murdered, then the bad guys will make it look like an accident and I'm fine, but if the authorities see that I was checking on the policy, then what? I decided that I couldn't look at the policy or even check to see if I was current. I was sure I was current, because I've always been current with everything, but I wasn't remembering my days. If my body was a temple and I destroyed that temple, wouldn't it be wrong for me to destroy the temple?[59] If I killed myself, it would because of those trying to get me and in essence, they would be have killed me. Was I the murderer or were they the murderers? Things were getting confusing.

My head was buzzing with the pain of the situation, I heard myself saying aloud, "Will you forget me forever? How long will you hide your face from me? How long must I take counsel in my soul and have sorrow in my heart all the day? How long shall my enemy be

---

[59] 1Cor. 3:17

exalted over me?"[60] At least I believe I was saying this out loud. I wasn't quite sure at the time, voices and thoughts were one as they tend to become in times of desperation.

I needed to figure this thing out and on my own. I couldn't have any more people with knowledge talking to me or knowing that I knew something. I couldn't have them knowing that I knew. Nothing was making sense.

My phone buzzed and there was a voice mail. I didn't know it had been ringing. I hadn't left my room in a while. I always paid my credit card off each month, so I had enough credit to stay at that lousy hotel for an indefinite period of time. I could stay there forever, but people knew I was there. I began to question whether I should have been moving about or staying in the room. I wondered whether I should just go and get a tent and live in a park somewhere until this all blew over. Then nobody would find me, but if they did, nobody would know I was dead. If nobody knew I was dead, then my wife would have to wait longer on the insurance. It takes a long time to declare someone dead if they are just missing. I thought living as a wanderer wouldn't do.

I looked at my phone…I did not recognize the number. Nothing bad could happen if I listened to the voicemail. But if the voicemail was something bad, it might screw with my head and my plans. Sometimes you perform better if you are naïve because you're less likely to hesitate. The accidents on those big diving boards always happened when people try and stop themselves at the last minute instead of letting their momentum take them.

A Texas Ranger had called me. An actual Texas Ranger. I knew they were real, but something about the concept seemed fictitious. He said he wanted to ask me a few questions and

---

[60] Psalm 13:1-2

would get in touch with me. He didn't say to call him back, but he left his number. I put my phone down and must have fallen asleep because time seemed to skip again.

I woke up to my phone buzzing once more. I thought I'd been asleep for a few hours, but it was only about five minutes. I didn't recognize this number either. I wanted to let this one go to voicemail as well, but I was anxious. I felt like I should have answered the phone when the Ranger called. When I heard his voicemail, I felt a bit of reassurance although such feelings were still framed in apprehension, as they have been since this ordeal began. I read somewhere once to always pick up the phone, even if it's a call you dread. I gathered this was to serve two purposes, to avoid missing any potential opportunities and to tackle the difficult calls without delay. I also read that you should always let the calls go to voicemail in order to appropriately prepare for such a difficult conversation, thus taking the surprise out of the whole matter. I wasn't sure which advice was the best.

Because I had already adhered to voicemail philosophy, I decided to answer the call before a message could be left. It was Mr. Carlisle, so the lesson was to always let the call go to voicemail.

"What do you want?" I asked, my voice breaking just a bit.

"You sound terrible. I assume you're not holding up so well are you?" Mr. Carlisle asked, sounding as genuinely concerned as he could. I didn't respond.

"Well, we need to meet. I'll come by and pick you up," he said.

"Nope, we're not doing that. I've got no interest in meeting you," I was weary and I knew he was an enemy.

"I don't understand. I'm the guy that can help you. You know me. If you think the law is going to help you you're wrong. They're in on it and they're taking out all the eyeballs that

95

have seen anything. Then they're going to come after the rest of us. Then eventually, they'll go down too. We're all going to the same place son…unless you and I do something about it," Mr. Carlisle abruptly hung up the phone.

I stared at the ceiling and began to take inventory of its irregularities. If a hotel is worn enough, there are some strange things going on above your head. Water stains that form some sort of Rorschach blots to be scrutinized by your inner thoughts. You ended up this way because you weren't hugged enough or hugged too much, depending on the situation. Your parents were too good, they didn't challenge you or were too absent, they needed to be there to pick you up when you fell accept when they shouldn't, because coddling leads to narcissism, which in turn leads to an unfulfilled life because a narcissist will never find satisfaction in any setting. But what is satisfaction? Are you supposed to be satisfied? Aren't you supposed to be content in your place in life? But you shouldn't be content because that leads to mediocrity, which is unacceptable and a sign of someone with a lack of ambition. I heard someone say once that good can become better and better can become best. Does "best" cease to exist if we all become "best"? If we are all rich, doesn't the value of the dollar diminish? If we are all the "best" then there can be no "best" and we are all "average" because "best" became merely "average". Doesn't "best" always step aside for "better"? We cannot all be rainmakers can we? There is not enough resources for us all to make it rain. It's impossible because we must take some rain from others in order to make it rain because there is not enough rain to go around. Now there is great gain with contentment, for we brought nothing into the world, and we cannot take anything out of the world.[61] But if we have food and clothing, with these we will be content.[62]

---

[61] 1 Tim. 6:6-7
[62] 1 Tim. 6:8

That ceiling was not perfect. In fact, it was mediocre to below mediocre at best. It had a water stain right by the air conditioning vent. It also had a spot that was clearly patched at one point in time. I never would have noticed these deficiencies if I weren't exhausted, frightened and unsure of my own reality, which is what forced me to flop down on the bed and stare at the ceiling in a state of catatonic rest. If that ceiling were perfect and all the other ceilings were perfect, would I have noticed? Not likely and even less likely if my circumstances were perfect. Now, from that day forward, I would subconsciously be observing and judging all ceilings which crossed my path.

When one's mind begins to wander about the implications of ceiling imperfections, it's an indication that one needs to leave their room. I wasn't sure if I had any clean clothes, I brought a couple suits thinking I would be in and out of the place after my initial interview with Jairo. I didn't account for the need for a washing machine or a dry cleaner. Although exhausted, my only physical activity during this time was driving, talking, meeting and fretting. I threw on some pants, a typical white shirt and assumed my coat and pants were matching. I didn't bother to shave or anything else for that matter and headed out to the rental car.

I thought I would at least drive around town, get to know the place, maybe find a local restaurant and get some Tex-Mex. I thought it was morning.

The Valley was so typical, yet so different. It always seemed windy and hot. Always hot. Not the kind of hot where it was just dead air, where the heat was just trapped down at your level. No, the wind moved and the air was dry, but the sun was just directly on you, scorching you, penetrating through your jacket. Nobody went anywhere without sweating. You leave your car, you go inside and get blasted by the cold air conditioning and you're drenched. You drive along and everything seems the same, no landmarks. No building appeared to be built before the eighties, but none of them seemed in that good of condition either. Strip center after strip center looked relatively new, but their parking lots all had weeds coming through the cracks. Cracks were in new construction. Decay of the new, that's all I saw. Billboards were everywhere advertising healthcare facilities or at home care, dialysis or something about health. It seemed like the entire world must be here to get healed, yet half the parking lots were empty. Nothing made sense to an outsider.

Palm trees with no beaches, surrounded by green fields and scrub. Green fields in an air that seemed dryer than a desert. You drove on that highway and you would see chain restaurant after chain restaurant, speckled with a few cabarets and healthcare facilities. Cracked empty parking lots were everywhere. Everything seemed upside down to me. I remember even the airport had a covered walkway that stretched almost all the way from the airport to the rental car parking lot, but for some reason just stopped short, right after an entire empty section of the airport. It had shoe shine people, but no working plugs for your phone or computer. Everyone spoke English, but there were Spanish signs everywhere. The people at the hotel, restaurants, everywhere for that matter were the friendliest people I have ever met in this country, yet murder, fraud and corruption were part of the air you breathed. But, the people were friendly. Why?

I found a little local restaurant. I was hungry. I sat down and asked the waitress for migas and coffee. They tasted great, although I'm not sure how much they compared to others. I was hungry, they were on my plate, so it seemed like they were great. Someone left a paper in the booth across the way from me. It's not often that you still see a paper lying around, but it was there, it might be the restaurant's. I skimmed through it, I saw nothing of the deaths or any deputies being suspended. It was as if the incident never occurred. I didn't bother trying to talk to anyone, as I got the feeling that they wouldn't talk.

I heard the chimes of the door ring and glancing up from my eggs and paper I saw a worn pair of boots lope inside. Deliberate, not in a hurry, but completely confident. The white straw cowboy hat tipped to the waitress, who showed no signs of knowing him. I thought he might be the Ranger. He seemed like a man of authority. I all of a sudden became nervous at the thought of conversing with him…I wasn't ready yet.

I casually stood up and made my way to the men's room to hide out in the stall. I would wait all morning if necessary. It's not that I completely didn't want to speak with this man, I just wasn't sure if I trusted him. I was pulled towards him mentally and possibly emotionally, as he represented one of the few people that might actually be able to help me. My thinking was that while the FBI might potentially be immune to the local corruption, they would immediately grill the family and disrupt those around me. The Rangers don't have the federal government behind them, so they aren't going to be swarming all over the place, busting up the wedding china. I thought that it was possible for the Ranger to be out of the bribery net as he was bound by the state and not the city or county. However, most of these theories held no water as I was well aware that plenty of federal border agents were bribed into looking the other way when a cartel had a shipment coming through. Really, the only people I could trust besides myself would be other victims or witnesses like Rudy Garza and Robin Keller…for however long any of these folks would remain alive.

I sat in the stall, perusing my phone to kill time. I would give it an hour tops before the Ranger left the place. The thought also occurred to me that the man was just a regular guy wearing a hat and boots, which is more common than not around here. Why did I assume he was a ranger? Do rangers even wear boots and cowboy hats? Did I just make some sort of assumption based on my own cultural knowledge? It didn't matter. I decided it wasn't worth the risk. I decided that I would wait him out.

After about ten minutes the bathroom door swung open. Those boots came scuffing in, took care of business and sauntered over to the sink to wash up. I watched under the stall as the boots turned toward me and faced me for some time. In a controlled deep growl of a drawl, a voice echoed, "Martin…come on out and talk to me when you finish up. I'll be in the booth towards the back. You can face the door if you feel nervous. I'm going to get a coffee and wait. Take however much time you need before you come see me. We need to come up with a way out, but I can't force you or ask you to do anything you don't want to do. Here's the thing son…I'm a ranger…they're them, we're us. The eyes can't say to the hand, 'I don't need you' and the head can't say to the feet, 'I don't need you.'[63] We need to work as one against them, you understand?[64] I'll be waiting for you."

The voice was gone and the boots casually walked out of the bathroom. I sat in the stall, playing with my phone, convincing myself I was reading or searching for something. It was just an act of comfort while I tried to figure out what I wanted to do. It seemed like I was just delaying the inevitable.

I believed the man when he said he was going to wait. The gravity of my situation was thoroughly appreciated, given my lack of sleep and horrid appearance, but my behavior was silly. A slight relief came over me in that the choice to meet with the Ranger was not given, but dictated. I didn't need to agonize over the situation. Even if he wasn't a ranger, I still had to

---

[63] 1Cor. 12:21
[64] 1Cor. 12:27

meet with this man as there was no escape. When given no good choice, it is comforting to have the choice made for me. I person just needed to deal with the situation and face it.

I washed my hands and headed to the dining area. There he was. You could pick him out of a novel or a movie. Worn boot cut jeans hanging over his equally worn boots, a thick, button up work shirt with a silver-star and hat still on his head, looking down at the paper. The guy had to be six foot three; was broad shouldered, no gut. He was a worker. He didn't come home and sit on the couch at night. He was sun darkened under that hat, with a bit of well cut salt and peppered hair showing below, and he had that mustache; it was a big silvered mustache, just like I imagined. He fit the mold, yet he still appeared abstract to me.

He caught my eye and nodded for me to sit down. I sat down across from him and we were silent for a moment while he appeared to be finishing that article he was pretending to read. Most likely, he was gathering his thoughts, getting ready to convince me to be a witness of some kind…how the risk was worth it because I would be saving lives and so forth. I wouldn't expose him on this though. It was always better to not let the other person know I was on to them, it kept them loose. I couldn't believe that I had come to a point in my life where I was thinking in such a manner…strategizing conversations, scheming to get an upper hand on who…an actual Texas Ranger or possibly someone connected to a drug cartel?

The Texas Rangers had an interesting and checkered history. The historical perception ranged from clean living heroes to criminals with badges. The matanza occurred in 1915. It was the result of an uprising against some of the racial segregation between whites and those of Mexican heritage when the railroad came to prominence in the Valley. There was a group that wanted an independent republic separate from the states. These insurgents were hard to track and a death list was created to take out those who were part of the insurgency and those suspected of helping it. The Texas Rangers were not particularly detailed as to whom they killed, which resulted in the slaughter being referred to as the matanza.

Times had changed and there was a chance that a ranger could be more resistant to corruption than the local groups. It would be hard to know either way.

The Ranger breathed heavy while putting down his newspaper, as if to convince me that he'd read something sad or annoying or really serious, I couldn't determine which feelings he was trying to convey. Once again, I was tempted to call him out on his fake reading of his fake article with his fake reaction. I thought I should ask him about the article, just to see what he came up with on the fly, but he started talking before I could even finish my thoughts on the matter.

"Six dead on the River Huerta. Someone told me that yesterday. I've got a contact down at the river, I won't tell you which side he's on, but he calls it the River Huerta. He's got a complete different perspective of the Rio Grande than others…I guess everyone does. It's a barrier for some, it protects others, its income and a symbol for most. This guy…he's not even seeing it in those terms, he's there with others that don't even recognize Mexico or the States or Texas…he talks about this other guy Huerta, says he runs the place. Heck, the Zeta's and the Gulf Coast guys didn't really know much about this Huerta fella. It's like he's a myth. But they work with him anyway, so I hear. My contact treats him like he's real and that it's this Huerta guy's river. I wonder if it's superstition? Anyway, after the incident with the OTM's getting lit on fire, your Jairo Ortiz kid died from burns or smoke…we all assume. That was the kid you were going to help right? Then you hear of another victim passing away, probably from the burns, I guess…who really knows the actual cause of death for anybody these days? Then you hear of another, or someone else going missing. Then you don't hear much anymore, do you?

People are gone, not showing up at work. Nobody else confirmed dead. This contact of mine says 'six dead on the River Huerta'. He's always been right, he's always around, always a part of things. He says they got buried. I don't know if this guy saying that six are dead on the river is related to our incident or not, people probably die all the time near the river and we don't know about it. I'm pretty sure that you don't know much about all this, other than what has happened to you. I can tell you this…they will get to your family, they will get to you and all those around you unless you come to me. I'm not saying that I have all the answers, because I don't. I'm the best shot you've got though," he paused and let his little speech linger for a bit, hoping that I digested it properly.

The Ranger reached his hand across the table for a shake, "Sorry about that Martin, I'm Regional Commander Torres of the Texas Rangers." I couldn't imagine turning down a handshake, so I took his hand and shook it out of obligation. Although, it was a bit awkward as he had offered his right and I reached over with my left for some reason, which ended up being one of those handshakes one might expect to receive from one's grandmother due to an arthritic condition of some kind. It did not go unnoticed by the Ranger as he raised one eyebrow in surprise. I understood, this was a simple action, which I made difficult through nerves and lack of sleep. I had also just confirmed to him that I was weak and tired.

We sat there looking at each other again in silence, waiting for the awkwardness to wash away. He was calm, collected and seemingly able to wait forever. Me, I was nervous and twitching, hoping for things to come to a head, tired of anticipating the worst and not knowing what would actually be the worst.

"In America…and Texas for that matter, as they are at times both one and the same to a certain extent, but different in a lot of ways…most of us from here know that this great state could survive without the other looking over us and pretending to take care of us…in this state and country…we are taught from a very young age how admirable it is to pull yourself up by your own boot straps. The rugged individualist is a virtue, right? That's what we think, what we know…and so on. Texas was an independent nation. My own ancestors were here before Texas was a nation…my family fought as many revolutions as you can imagine. We fought Spain to become Mexico, and we fought Mexico to become Texas. Lives were lost, blood was shed and landscapes changed…for independence. It was all about freedom, being able to run a nation the way we wanted, on our own without some sovereign looking over our shoulder. Independence son! That's what it's all about. We don't want to ask for help because it's shameful. Now what do we do about all those beggars sitting there at the median with their signs, asking for money over there in the big cities? It's a shame isn't it? That's no way to go through life, begging for help from someone else stronger and in a better spot in life. When you need help and ask for help, don't you lose your independence…your freedom if you will? Don't those that help you start to mold your will and character to that for which they desire? If you rely on yourself and not others, don't you get to control the outcome…get to do things your way, the right way…am I right?" Regional Commander Torres paused after he finished and looked around for a bit, appearing to be checking out the other patrons. He looked me up and down over that grand silver mustache, watching my reaction, waiting for a sign that I could be molded by him.

The Ranger continued, "Them kids of yours…that little boy and girl…you're trying to resolve this mess, so they don't have to suffer the consequences. Same with your lovely wife…if you put your mind to it, you can get through this without disturbing that family of yours. The kids may just think this is a neat weeklong stay at grandma's while daddy is away, then you come back home, things have been fixed and nobody is the wiser, their life can continue as it always had before. You've provided the best life you can for them and will continue to do so, am I right?"

I looked at him, waiting for the payoff. This long speech, this preachy garbage that presumed I was weak and he was strong. I was fed up with people trying to dictate my course of action based on some sort of perceived weakness. Who was this guy…a ranger? So what. What was so different between the two of us to convince him that he can play mind games with me? Mr. Carlisle tried the same thing. What was the difference between this "good guy" ranger and that scumbag Mr. Carlisle? I assumed he was a scumbag, but by this point, I couldn't determine who was on my side and who wasn't. The seed of my irritation was basically about this constant need for some perceived authority figure to attempt to mentally break me down in an effort to push me in a direction, as if it was simply a matter of executing some psychological or negation technique that only they know about. As if it was just a matter of knowing the right move and executing it, like I had no say in the matter. I felt like I was smarter than this guy. Intellect wasn't necessarily reflected in power or wealth. There were plenty of people born rich and plenty of imbeciles that obtained some sort of power. Rich did not equal smart. Authority is not a reflection of intellect.

I could tell that the Ranger sensed that he overplayed his hand and believed he needed to dial things back again. I did him no good if we were adversaries. He needed me to talk and participate in some form. He knew it and I knew it.

Ranger Torres grumbled and breathed heavy again, as if this whole episode were a burden. He sipped his coffee, exhaled with exaggerated pleasure, just like Mr. Carlisle did with his booze, and he continued, "I get it. You're insulted… and you should be, at least at first. You've got to understand that this whole thing is bigger than you. Hell, any reasonable person would know that, son. You've got potential cartel involvement, maybe even the big ones you've read about…if they're still round in that area. It's hard to keep up with it all, there always seems to be a power vacuum these days. Martin, we're talking about folks that don't have a code…no ethics! The old guard was bad, but these guys will kill kids…in a bad way, so we all remember and have nightmares at night about what we saw or even heard. It's not the Wild West, it's more like an apocalypse, the end of days, when people are starving and cannibalizing each other, that sort of thing. Do you know what I mean by that? We're not talking about people trying to rob you or you getting caught in a cross fire, we're talking about a degradation of humanity here, where people are no longer people, but animals or monsters, where they just assume kill you as sneeze if you're lucky, we're talking about the red horse swooping down. If they want some sort of entertainment, they rape and light people on fire…that's what they do for fun, not because they need to send a message of brutality or anything, but because they just might be bored. We are dealing with people that view you no differently than a roach. Your son and daughter's screams would be meaningless to them, like a breeze or a bird chirping. I'm talking about a trumpet blaring and hail and fire mixed with blood thrown down on the earth, one third of us set on fire, one third of the trees burned and all the green grass burned to a crisp![65]"

He could see that none of this was registering with me. I had already heard similar things from Mr. Carlisle and he tried to convince me to handle it on my own and now this guy is using the same fear tactics to convince me not to handle the matter on my own. So which way was it? Was I supposed to handle things myself and perpetuate some sort of violent cartel retribution or should I go to the authorities and have the same result?

---

[65] Rev. 8:7

If I went to the authorities, I would for sure bring things to the forefront and it would not be a matter of whether someone wanted to kill me and my family, rather it would be a matter of whether I could be protected. Could a sometimes elite, sometimes corrupt and sometimes bumbling government entity protect me or even be willing to protect me from these animals? Or, would I be able to handle things and slip under the radar until the whole thing blows over? All I knew for sure was that I was at least a known commodity. I knew what I was capable of doing and I could at least somewhat control things or have some input into my fate. If I sought help from this ranger or anyone else for that matter, then I more or less relinquish all control. The Ranger could be bought or even killed himself…then what? There would be activity around me, which would put me in the open and I would surely be found. If the government can't keep a lunatic off the White House lawn who was threatening to shoot the President, then how would I be protected? No, there was too much of an unknown to go to the authorities. I had to walk away.

Ranger Torres could tell that he was losing me and gave me what appeared to be a last ditch pitch. He didn't even bother looking up at me this time around; he just stared at his worn hands folded as if in prayer. He spoke with an old dog's growl, "I don't need you…I'd like to have you on my side, but I don't need you. I will survive. You're not the first fella I've tried to help who has turned me down. You know what they say, 'Don't throw your pearls to swine'[66] or something like that. I'm not trying to offend your or anything, but if you don't know the value of a pearl and are…frankly upset that I'm trying to give a pearl, then what else can I really do for you? I've got to do my due diligence. I can't let you step out in front of a freight train without trying to stop you, right? What kind of person would I be if I didn't at least try? Really, I'm

---

[66] Matt. 7:6

probably obligated to try a few times or I won't be able to sleep at night I assume. Woe to me if I don't, right?[67] However, I can't force it and after a while, you just have to let a person go and focus on tasks that can actually be accomplished. All I can do is preach the word; be ready in season and out of season; reprove, rebuke, and exhort, with complete patience.[68] Maybe I can help some more of those victims. Maybe I can find out what happened to that game warden…"

"What?" I could barely get the meek question out of my mouth. My chest was tightening and a bit of panic washed over my being.

The Ranger looked up sharply, he could see that this information had struck a cord. He sat looking me in the eye and paused in a exaggerated manner before answering so he could make sure the gravity of what he said would sink into me.

"Yep. She's gone. That's one of the reason's I'm down here. Lady named Robin Keller. I'm assuming she's dead, but you got to go through the process and find out if she can be saved before you call it," Ranger Torres explained. He sighed and looked around a bit, then the expression on his face changed from concerned to anger as he continued, "You know what pisses me off sometimes? I know I should care about you, but the fact of the matter is, you are keeping me from finding her! You can save yourself, you know information, you can help others, but you don't seem inclined. That young game warden…she was just ending her rounds like she's always done, every day. I'm thinking someone knew it, like they wanted her to see something. She did and now she's paying the price. She's dead or missing or whatever just because she happened to be alive and doing her job at a particular spot and time. She wasn't a threat, she was a pair of eyes to witness a disaster. Then, for that very reason, she is in trouble. She called it in, just like she was supposed to do. She didn't think about whether she could handle it herself,

---

[67] 1 Cor. 9:16
[68] 2 Tim. 4:2

whether she was affecting anyone else or even if she was in danger. She knew what was right and she did it…because that's what she was supposed to do. She didn't get a chance to waiver back and forth and turn down good intentioned people trying to help her. Nope, she's gone and I'm getting angrier and angrier thinking about what a fool I am trying to help a fool like you. Here's my card, call me when you figure out the right thing to do. In the meantime, I'll be doing what I can for those that want some help. Maybe some of those burn victims might appreciate it if I get this thing resolved. Victims need folks on their side that will get their hands dirty a bit, and get in the muck with them. Not some lawyer running around trying to protect his own interests. Martin…I am flawed. Just like you and everyone else. If I'm being honest, you would know that at some point I will let you down, just like you'll let me down and we'll both let others down. It's inevitable. I'm not perfect. But despite those flaws and me occasionally going off track, I know that there are greater things in life than looking after myself. I know that despite my job as a ranger and my appearance…I know that you've got to do things for the sake of loving the rest of the world. You can speak all the languages of the world, but if you don't love others, you'd only be a noisy gong or a clanging symbol.[69] Do you understand, Martin? There's nothing wrong with the instinct of self-preservation. It's engrained in us. We were born with it. It's natural. But we're not kids anymore. When we were kids, we spoke, thought and reasoned like kids. But we grew up and we must put away childish things.[70] It's time to think differently Martin."

My face got hot and my temper flared up, which was a bit abnormal for me, but these were abnormal circumstances. I was tired of being talked down to and it was time for me to be heard, "I guess maybe I do need to start thinking differently…not so sure either way anymore.

---

[69] 1 Cor. 13:1
[70] 1 Cor. 13:11

Not really sure who I can trust to be honest…you? Do I trust you? Just because you say you're the way, doesn't make you the way. I know I can't take on a cartel, I'm not an idiot. You do realize that don't you? You realize that I'm not an idiot…correct? Not every idiot can become a lawyer and do well at a top firm, you understand? Know your audience before espousing your well planned speeches. You're a smart guy and maybe you have more experience than me…having been through more situations and so on, so you can apply a few tricks of the trade and get a couple of little victories here and there, but you're not smarter than me! You might be wiser, but you're not smarter. There's a difference! I know when you're applying a tactic and it's insulting. If you need me to help be a part of whatever means you have to an end, just ask and I'll consider it, but don't use tactics on me! Insulting me will not prompt me to help you. Your need for me to be some sort of witness does not, I repeat, does not need to be guised in some sort of fake altruistic concern for my wellbeing!"

I was tired of it all. Tired of people pushing me around, tired of people trying to use me, tired of people telling me the ways of the world and certainly tired of people talking down to me. I didn't know where I was headed or who was right, but was not going to do anything without letting everyone know that I could not be pushed around.

Regional Commander of the Texas Rangers, J.C. Torres looked at me unblinking took a breath and said, "Here's the thing about the river, Martin, it's hard to figure out what's real and what's not. I hear stories about a couple of guys that hang out around there. I've heard about them since I've been working this area, but I've never seen them…personally. I've seen the results of their actions, but no personal physical sign of their existence, but I believe they exist because I see signs of them all around me. One seems to concentrate on good things, the other seems to enjoy trying his hand in the bad."

110

The Ranger took another sip of his coffee and continued, "The bad one is a guy named Huerta; he's the one that my contact says runs the river. He either lives by the river or on the river or visits the river from time to time…I don't know the details. I've never seen him, but I think he exists because I've heard enough about him. My understanding is that he always seems to be involved with these type of things, like a facilitator. Problem is that nobody can catch him or pin him on any of this type of stuff and he's not really the boss of a cartel or anything. Like I said, he's more like a facilitator or an instigator. The people that come in contact with him always seem to describe him differently. One person says he's dirty another says he's clean, you get the picture. Heck, I don't even know if he's American or Mexican or OTM. That's the thing…I've spoken with county commissioners, justices of the peace, border patrol guys…the ones who've taken bribes, and a good chunk of them had contact with this Huerta fella. Not always directly, sometimes it was through someone else who had links to him, but he's just around, always comes up. The thing is…he gets involved in small things just as much as big things. A low level border patrol guy took a tiny bribe and implicated this Huerta. At the same time, I remember a few years ago there was a murder attempt on some county attorney and the suspect said it was Huerta. Maybe he's a red hearing, you know like someone to blame even if we don't see them or catch them. We're talking about direct links to a couple thousand dollars as well as a potential murder of a government official. Both incidents seemed to have the same level of involvement with this Huerta guy. I don't even know what the guy looks like, but here's what's real interesting, nobody thinks he's important enough to pursue, but everyone seems to implicate him! As far as I know, he doesn't care about borders, he works on both sides and has no affiliation with either country. A buddy of mine down here that works in local law enforcement told me about debriefing an illegal he picked up one time. When my buddy asked the guy to give some details about how he crossed the Rio Grande, the illegal corrected him and called it the 'Rio Huerta'. Now what do you suppose I'm supposed to make of Huerta? I can't ignore him because even if I don't think he's real, his name seems to be involved in everything that goes wrong…so to a certain extent, he has to be real. Right? A lot of these cartel guys post pictures of all their riches and girls online for the world to see. It's a machismo thing. This Huerta, assuming he exists, seems to relish in the fact that nobody knows he's real or not. I think, deep down inside, he enjoys just causing problems and chaos. I could just assume see him turn against the cartel just to cause catastrophe. That's my character profile of Huerta, he just enjoys bad. Point being, you keep this up and you'll probably run into him or someone claiming to work on his behalf and that's not going to be good."

The Ranger looked off a bit, lost in thought, then he chuckled to himself and said, "Listen to me…I gave you a character profile of someone who I've never seen. That's the thing though, he's had such an impact that I have to treat him like he's real and I will. What other choice do I have? What's interesting is that there's this other guy I hear about too…Banez. Banez, tends to come up when people talk about being helped out at the river or rescued and what not. So, my guess is that he's a good guy, but I sometimes hear bad things about Banez as well. Regardless, Huerta and Banez, somehow that correlates with good and evil in my mind. I don't know if I'm right, like I said, I never physically met either one of them."

I thought this was interesting. Before, the Ranger was speaking about myths, now he's actually trying to tell me something factual. I had pretended to be too distracted to listen through most of his story, but now he saw that he peaked my interest. I was disappointed in myself for having such a terrible poker face. It followed that my disappointment was proportionate to the Ranger's encouragement to continue.

Ranger Torres went deeper into his story, "I was investigating a matter several years ago, which was the first and last time I that I was tempted to take a gift. It wasn't even that much, it never is really, nobody becomes a millionaire by taking bribes. The bad guys are just as cash conscious as anyone else. So, they try to feel out who's vulnerable and get them on the cheap. The bad guys find the weakest link and exploit it, there's no point in overpaying. You find a judge or border guy with money troubles, problems or a professional grafter, you know the kind that take lots and lots of smaller gifts. You take one big bribe and you're done. Sometimes it's money, sometimes maybe someone knows someone else who needs some consulting work or contract work done on a build out…that sort of thing. You know when you see some middle of the road government official all of a sudden have a bunch of landscaping done on their house? That's when they took a bribe. Landscaping here or there, maybe an unusual amount of toilet paper shows up, no money trail. Anyway, I was lower level, we just had our kids and I just got back from an Indian Casino in Louisiana. I made a mistake and had some big bills to pay. Looking back, it was nothing you or I couldn't eventually manage, but when you're young and don't have anything, it's a daunting task. Everyone around me was doing better then me, everyone. Some the right way, many the wrong, but they were all doing better."

Ranger Torres rubbed his temple, as if he was back at that spot in his life. Memory of that time clearly had a visceral effect on him. He took a breath and continued, "Anyway, those guys can sniff you out when things seem tough. They smell desperation. They seem to have the answer or at least provide what appears to be answers. When you are longing for a solution, they show up and give it to you. You need hope and it looks like they are that hope. It may cost you everything, but at that moment in time, you just want a short term solution and they have it. Well, I can tell you that I stayed clean, but I gave just enough of a hesitation to cause someone to approach and once they approach, you have a conflict and once you have a conflict, someone has to pay. They don't leave you alone, even if you don't want to participate...you see? Once they find out that they've misjudged you and made a mistake, then things get even more dangerous. Long story short, I stood my ground and said no to their advances, which meant that I was in big trouble. Instead of doing the right thing and seeking extra help, I ignored the matter. I ignored it because I didn't do anything wrong in my mind. So if I didn't do anything wrong, why would anything bad happen to me? Right? Isn't that how the world works? You're a good person and bad things don't happen to you. Well, I don't have to tell you that I was wrong. You know that yourself. Bad things can happen to good people and good things can happen to bad people. The sun rises on the evil and on the good, and rain is sent on the just and on the unjust.[71]"

The Ranger stopped for a moment and seemed to be struggling to compose himself, he took a breath and continued, not looking at me anymore, just staring at the wall, "I was young, my wife was young. She was young. Then she was gone. Vanished. I never saw her again. It's almost worse than seeing someone you love die...not knowing. But she was gone. I knew the moment she didn't come home from work on time that she was gone. You could set your watch to her. That's when I decided to get help, but they were watching me. There was a whole group of them. They took me to the river, made me dig a hole to put my body in, put me on my knees, and then popped me in the back of the head. I blacked out. I have no idea what happened, but as I was coming to, I felt safe. I saw just a man...everyone else was gone. I was just lying there on the soft sand. The man had wrapped up my head and gave me some water. He looked dirty, like he was a hermit or something living out there, that's what I'd assumed at least. He hummed melodically the whole time I was clearing my head. He was blurry, but I could hear him clearly.

---

[71] Mat. 5:45

He said I was safe. I fell asleep again and when I woke up the next morning, it was just me on the sand with the birds. It seemed like a dream, but my head was wrapped. Somebody had saved me, but I couldn't clearly see him. I've always thought it was that man they called Banez, but I can't outright prove it. Martin, what I'm trying to say here is that there are elements around the river that make no sense to you or anyone else that's not been around it. We live by rules, borders, fences and ethics. There are others that don't see things the same. That border is meaningless to some…languages hold no barriers and sovereign authority is just something designated by a piece of paper somewhere."

The Ranger looked into my eyes again, trying to figure out if any of this was penetrating. I was too tired, too disheveled to care. I was being driven by my body, by my will without contemplation of things beyond my immediate concerns. I nodded silently to him, just to get the Ranger to move on with his day.

"Martin, did you ever hear about Rio Rico?" I shook my head and Ranger Torres continued, "Not many people have. The Treaty of Guadalupe said that the main Rio Grande river bed would serve as the boundary between Mexico and the United States. The problem is that back then, if you wanted to divert the river for your farm land or for whatever reason, you would just dynamite or dig out a section and divert the whole damn river to fit your needs. You get your irrigation water and so on, but you also completely change the border. You can imagine the problems then, can't you? At some point in time, I think it was in the 1880's, they amended the treaty to clarify that only natural changes to the river would be a recognized change of the border. A few years later, about 1907 or so, an American irrigation company built a pumping building near a real extreme bend in the river. The land is arid down here, so you have temperatures that can grow crops year round, just not enough rain. So if you could be on the

115

ground floor and build yourself an irrigation business, you're making some good money. So the powers that be saw this bend as a potential problem in that if there was a flood of some kind, that whole portion of the river could be pushed up to a mile away. So what does an enterprising irrigation company do to insure they don't lose the resource, and to not violate a treaty between the United States and Mexico? You wait until dark and blast the hell out of the land with dynamite until the river bend is no more and you have a nice straight river close to you pumping building, that's what you do! Well, as you can imagine, there were a bunch of farmers that went to bed in the U.S. and woke up the next day in Mexico and without water for their crops. The company got sued by a bunch of folks, had to pay fines and was forced to pay for new boundary markers. Not surprisingly, the company never did mark the US/Mexico border, which was now on the other side of the river because the river course was changed by man! Eventually the whole matter was forgotten!"

"Why are you telling me this?" I asked.

"Wait, I'm getting to the interesting stuff," said the Ranger. "You see, eventually there was this town, Rio Rico in Mexico. It built a walking bridge across the Rio Grande during prohibition. Americans would come down to whatever American border town was there, pay a fee to get across the river on the walking bridge, and go get hammered without breaking any laws. Then they'd just stumble back across, go to sleep, wake up and do it again the next day until they were out of money. Eventually Rio Rico moved, due to flooding and such and was part of the forgotten tract south of the river that was actually American. After prohibition ended, Rio Rico didn't serve much of a purposes especially after the bridge was washed away. It basically became another Mexican town. It had Mexican schools, Mexican police, Mexican laws and Mexican roads. So it was an American town, south of the Rio Grande and maintained by

116

Mexico. Sometime in the 1970's, a fella who was born in Rio Rico tried to immigrate to America. His immigration lawyer did some research and decided that his client was and has always been an American citizen because the American border was supposed to include this chunk just south of the Rio Grande. Well, it didn't work, which caused a big raucous. A few years later, the US ceded the land to Mexico, it was just easier that way, and this fella that wanted to immigrate was declared a U.S. citizen. So there you have it…that's Rio Rico."

I stared at this ranger, perplexed by his tale. Irritated that I had to sit through it all. I raised my voice, not falsifying any sort of politeness, not now at least, and said, "I still don't know why you told me this story. Why are you wasting our time?"

Ranger Torres looked at me, just as puzzled and answered curtly, "Because…who gives a shit? Son, this is all a big steamy pile of nothing. When everything hits the fan and we've all got to answer, none of this stuff matters! We're fighting, killing, smuggling, making rules, breaking rules, bribing, getting bribes, stumping, refuting, getting statistics, deporting, accepting and so forth because of a man made, self-actualizing border that has an underground economy stronger than most countries and is run by a group of people that don't give two flying shits about our treatises, walls, fences, languages, our lives or our families' lives and they especially don't give a damn about either of these countries and what these countries might have to say about the matter! In vain you rise early and stay up late, toiling for food to eat— for he grants sleep to those he loves.[72]"

The Ranger stood up and strolled off without saying another word or even looking back at me. I looked at his card and ordered a coffee. The food was good at this place…the coffee was terrible. I didn't like what Regional Commander Juan Carlos Torres or J.C. or Ranger

---

[72] Psalm 127:2

Torres or whatever he called himself had to say. I've done plenty of good in my life to where I don't need this guy telling me what I'm doing wrong. It'll never be good enough with these type of folks. He was either a self-righteous critic or a scammer. The whole thing could be garbage. He's trying to get me to talk, so he can resolve his case and move on…he's got no interest in helping me. He probably deals with this all the time…gains trust of a witness or criminal, gets statements, has them testify then gone, never to be heard from again. Case closed, move on to the next. I had no interest in being part of that guy's scheme. It was a nice speech, but it was a speech best reserved for those that have alternatives, those that are lost. I hadn't lost yet and didn't plan on it anytime soon.

I threw some money down on the table and left the café. I flipped the Ranger's card and noticed a handwritten note on the back that said, "A cord of three strands is not quickly broken.[73]"

I thought it was strange seeing as he must have prewritten it on the card before meeting me. He probably had a stack of cards that say something like that on the backs. Maybe he changed them up a bit to say something a little different each time, like a fortune cookie.

I was lost in thought until I noticed a black town car had pulled up and parked in front of me. The windows were tinted, there was nothing particularly descript about the car itself other than the fact that I had never seen a town car in South Texas. I'm not sure if I was even frightened by it, although appeared to be waiting specifically for me. The only other people in the café were a couple of old field hands and I doubt that those gentlemen had access to a car service.

I was tired and strained, but not frightened. In fact, I had reached the point where my lack of sanity was pushing me to closure instead of safety. I was tired of wondering if I'd be

---

[73] Eccl. 4:12

killed or kidnapped or go to jail or…bump into that ranger's ghost friends at the river. No, I wanted confrontation, I was too tired to guess at anything.

The blood rushed to my face as I marched swiftly to the blacked out car and banged on the window. I yelled at the unseen passenger to either show themselves or get lost, I can't quite remember what exactly was said because my mind was being driven by something beyond my conscious control. I was on autopilot for lack of a better description. I scratched and pounded on the window until it just opened a crack.

I stepped back in response and held my breath, waiting for whatever was to come next. After about half a minute I heard a voice. It sounded a bit like Mr. Carlisle, but I couldn't be sure of it. There was something muffled or garbled about the voice to keep me from identifying it one hundred percent.

"Hop in the car…Martin," was all the voice from the car said to me. I shook my head.

"Hop in the car," it said again. I slowly backed away.

"Martin…we know where they are and where they're going. It's not difficult to track people these days. She and the kids are either at her parents or on the way there. Your mother in law posted her excitement about seeing them online. She can't help it, she's just so excited," the voice was almost at a whisper and with no inflection.

Something took over me again and my lungs began to heave, as if I was hyperventilating. I whirled around looking for anything to grab, finding a loose brick. I picked up the brick, screamed something unintelligible and hurled it at the car as it sped away, turned a corner and disappeared. They clearly didn't want to draw attention to themselves and my behavior must have spooked them enough to leave.

119

My family…what kind of person was I? Why did I assume that they were out of any sort of danger? Worse, why hadn't I been thinking of them?

I needed to call my wife, but my phone was dead. I didn't know her number, so I couldn't call from the café. I didn't know my wife's phone number, she was just listed as a name on my phone, I never needed to know it. The absurdity of it all…I needed to go back to my hotel room just to charge a phone to call my wife and tell her she's in danger. This great technological advance in communications actually held me back from a simple phone call. I couldn't do it!

I hopped into the rental and raced off down the road back to the hotel. For the first time in my life that I can recall, I ran a red light narrowly missing two cars crossing the intersection, which I didn't know about until their screeching tires and honks caused me to glance in my rearview mirror. My eyes hurt and my sight was beginning to place things out of focus. I was manic, pressure was building in my ears and I was just running on blood being pumped rapidly through my body. In times of great stress, the intellectual prowess of a human becomes completely reduced to that of an animal. I was just reacting. I'm not sure how much sleep I'd had, I don't recall how long I'd been in the valley and I certainly didn't know how fast I was driving. Frankly, I didn't really know which direction either. All I wanted to do was get in contact with my wife and kids.

I wondered why I had pushed them out of my head for so long. It could have been an out of sight out of mind type of issue. In other words, people were missing, dying around me and threatening me, so I just wasn't naturally thinking of them. It seemed terrible, but possible. It wasn't a conscious effort, so I needed to deduce an explanation. It just sort of happened. I knew there were times in my life when my family, those I'm meant to love and hold close, were often reduced to burdens or projects. Things to be undertaken or dealt with in order to finish up some work, read or watch something on television. Like washing dishes…tucking my kids in bed so they can go to sleep and not distract me. Dealing with my wife's problems in order to end the discussion as opposed to actually helping her through love. On to the next thing was probably my mental state for most of my marriage. It was better than being alone for sure, but I certainly wasn't treating my family as a blessing. They were a burden and a distraction for a long time. Then suddenly they are completely pushed to the background as a side issue when this mess ensued. Now…through no fault of their own, my wife, kids, in-laws, parents and any other person that was acquainted with me were in extreme danger. This was not a moral dilemma, it was a duty. It was my duty to protect those innocent people around me.

The same question kept arising…how do I protect them? If I go to the authorities and the authorities are part of it, then it just meant that my family would be killed sooner rather than later. If I handled it myself, they were most likely doomed as well. I was just a lawyer, I had no power, no connections…nothing.

When you think of things beyond the road you are racing down, accidents will occur. It was inevitable. I either side swiped a car next to me or I was the one who was bumped, I couldn't really say for sure, but I was pushed off the road into a traffic signal pole, hard enough to set off my air bag.

I didn't feel any pain because my body must have been pumping a massive amount of adrenaline into my system. I knew the airbag had deployed and smashed my face because my left cheek and jaw were completely numb, which meant at some point pain would follow. I didn't want to touch any part of my body for fear of finding something that would cause alarm.

My only instinct was to get out of the car as fast as possible and run or crawl to safety. For all I knew, that car purposely hit me in order to take me out.

I was able to unbuckle my seat belt, my ears had an awful buzzing sound, which prevented me from hearing the crowd that was beginning to gather or the man wailing from the other car.

I wasn't sure if he was hurt or just acting. Maybe the other driver was legitimately hurt and he had a passenger that was going to finish the job or maybe they would just wait for another chance later. I didn't want to find out. I could feel my legs, which gave me a bit of relief, but I wasn't sure if I'd be able to walk. I pulled myself over to the passenger side and was able to pry the door open enough to pull myself out onto the sidewalk with a thud.

I could hear the drops of blood splatter on the ground…rapidly. It sounded like the garden hose spraying all over the driveway back home. Back home…what was happening? These are the situations you see in the movies, they don't happen in real life, but there I was, bleeding, people closing in around me, people trying to kill me. Were my wife and kids alive?

I tried to stand, but lost my balance and fell onto my shoulder. Someone shouted for me to relax, but I couldn't figure out who was helping and who was trying to hurt me. I didn't know anyone. I pushed some hands away and tried to stumble a bit more into the grass, away from the hands, but fell again.

I heard a car pull up quickly, through the buzzing in my head, the pain, the dizziness and the shouting. People began to back up, which made me feel slightly safer, then I heard a familiar voice call out to me and I stumbled towards it.

"Get in, I'll get you out of here," said the voice. The sun was blinding me, I couldn't make out a face, but I jumped into the car, just to get away. I'd rather take my chances with someone I knew rather than alone amongst the mob.

I hand pulled me in the back of the car, the door slammed shut and we were on our way. It was quiet and dark. I felt safe.

"Well, it looks like we're in this together after all old pal," the voice trailed off, I heard a bit of a chuckle as it all faded away. Mr. Carlisle had rescued me.

Chapter 9 – Huerta.

There was blurred movement about me as I began to open my eyes. I could tell that I wasn't in the car anymore. We must have reached a safe spot as I could hear some laughter and casual conversation in the background. It was warm, cozy and for some strange reason I felt a bit of safety for the first time since this whole ordeal began. There was some dirt underneath me, but it was dry, almost clean. Incense perfumed the air and thwarted the visibility. Orange flickering lights moved about on the walls from what seemed to be a fire somewhere. There were no windows, no outside light...like I was holed up in a den or a cave underground somewhere.

All that I could hear were muffled voices, talking calmly and sounding social. I heard my name a few times, or so I thought, as my mind was not fully operational. I tried to get up, but I couldn't move my legs or even my arms. I didn't feel pain, just numbness. Normally I would panic at the prospect of not being able to move my limbs, but a glow of satisfaction and contentment just seemed to roll over me like warm bathwater. I was in a den, surrounded by strangers, after a car wreck, yet I couldn't care less. Nothing mattered to me.

I wouldn't go so far as to say that I was in bliss, as I wasn't. I was comfortable, but there was an element of nausea about my being. My comfort and lack of any real concern about my surroundings was completely counterintuitive to my situation. If I were a third-party observer taking in the scene, I would determine that I needed to flee, but for some reason I remained.

As the haze began to clear a bit, I could see women and men lounging about on the dirt floor, smoke swirling from their mouths only to linger in the center of the flickering space. There seemed to be rugs here and there...some on the walls, others on the floor. It seemed dirty, like the room was thrown together with junk scavenged here and there. Yet, there seemed to be

124

some sort of theme from what I could tell through the haze. The room was arrayed in purple and scarlet, and adorned with some gold and jewels and pearls scattered about and what appeared to be a golden cup sat near the wall.[74]

A dog walked about, sniffing some of the people from behind, being careful not to touch them or approach from the front. It looked like a typical junkyard dog…a mutt missing bits of fur here and there, but this one had a full belly. The dog behaved in a calculated manner, even in my borderline hallucinogenic state. I could see that it was smart or at least crafty enough to stay alive. It didn't trust the humans, but stayed around because it knew there was food and shelter. This was its comfort zone. It wasn't free and there was always the potential for abuse, but it wouldn't go hungry or be cold. Out in the streets, that dog would need to compete, to fight for its food. It would be forced to move from one spot to another with no permanent shelter or square meal waiting for it, or so it would seem. Here, in this den of smoke and darkness, that dog stayed in the warm, dank room, that room with no outside light and just waited for the food to drop.

I watched that dog for what seemed to be an hour. My head was on the dirt floor, fading in and out of consciousness and watching that dog. That dog…going from one spot to the next, not making eye contact, but not really totally hiding from these people. I couldn't figure out what he was scared of as most of the people didn't seem interested in it. I couldn't figure out what I was scared of either. I was calm, content, but had that bit of fear tucked down in my belly. Maybe I was finally realizing that I couldn't move, that I was vulnerable. I was inside away from the car wreck, but wasn't secure like I felt when I was home.

---

[74] Rev. 17:4

That dog came slinking over to me and began skittishly nosing around my leg. I had a small wound, I could feel it. Dogs will come and lick a sick man's sores.[75] I moved ever so slightly and it jumped back quickly, scurrying away. A few moments later and I could feel its cold wet nose sniffing the back of my leg again. I shook and the dog jumped back. It must have sensed my weakness because that dog was not waiting very long between flight and investigation. It was like a gnat, not really harmful, but annoying and a bit menacing. I didn't think that dog would attack me, but it certainly would have eaten me if given the opportunity and the assurance that I would not fight back. This back and forth swatting and sniffing between the two of us went on for some time, while my vision began to clear up. I could have sworn that I saw Mr. Carlisle, but it wasn't him.

Shadows of people were cast about the cavern, milling around murmuring to each other. Some appeared to be in sexual provocations while others were chatting or smoking and some were just slumped over by themselves. They weren't loud, these voices from the forms of people, but constant. There was no silence. I couldn't distinguish any conversations, it just sounded like activity interrupted occasionally with a bit of laughter or a curse. The noise seemed to grow louder, like a rising tide or wall of sound, low boil that gets louder and louder until your heart beats a little faster. My breathing was getting heavy as the excitement seemed to increase, louder and louder until a voice cut through it all and commanded attention.

"You've got this guy over there, he said something the other day…I found it interesting. This American bigshot says the other day, he says the Mexican government is so smart and cunning that they send the bad ones, the rapists and criminals across the river over there. He says Mexico doesn't want to pay for them so it sends them over the river," he began to

---

[75] Luke 16:21

uncontrollably laugh at the prospect. Soon a roar of laughter followed his from the forms that moved and mingled about. I didn't know who he was talking to, but it sure seemed like it was directed at me. I couldn't find the source of the voice, but there was a familiarity to it and something about it that I could relate to, like this person was some long lost friend of mine.

"You listening mister lawyer…huh? He just sits there wriggling around on the ground like a worm or something," another round of laughter ensued. "You think the cartel would let Mexico send their folks across the river…my river? Nobody 'sends' anybody across my river without me allowing it, not Mexico, not anybody. Let me tell you something …you build that wall on my river, I'll knock it down and if I can't, I'm going under," the entire party cheered this strange retort that was apparently directed at me regarding something I had never said. It was bizarre really. He seemed to be lecturing me or chastising me.

"It doesn't matter, that guy doesn't care about that wall or the river. You know why? Because guys like me and him, we don't pay no regard to what any government says is a border or a wall or a barrier or a gate. If we want something that's locked up, we go get those bolt cutters and take it. It's not yours or theirs, it's all mine! That cartel…it don't care what Mexico says, what America says, what you say about where they can and can't go. They've got guys on both sides of that river. Mexico, the U.S…it makes no difference. We aren't citizens of any country. This is our world and we let you live in it. We let you draw up your pretend boundaries. The cartels don't care about that river, but they like it cause it makes them money. They're like you, just making money off something that isn't real. You're a lawyer, I know…a lawyer is a job that was created out of thin air. You know how I know? Cause when this world goes kaboom, a lawyer ain't going to help nobody. If you didn't have those laws written down, thought up from somebody's head, nobody would need a guy to read those laws for them. Just like that border. The world goes up in smoke, that border is worthless. You might as well make up your own alphabet, convince the world that they need that new alphabet, and make a job for someone to read it for everyone. That's what you are, a reader…that's all."

"Mr. Carlisle?" I was able to mumble. People laughed again.

"Who? I'm everything. I'm Huerta...maybe. I could be just the man that runs the show. A wolf. You and all those other people out there… you're all the little fleas that ride around on our backs. Me and the other wolves, we go back and forth across that river, we're strays, we're dogs of war. You jump off before we go across. That river… that line drawn on the map between those two countries, that's for you, not me and not him!" Huerta got up and walked over to me.

"It doesn't matter, I'm the guy that facilitates. I make things happen. I encourage. I give people like you doubt or build you up, whatever works best for me. This time around though…it's different. Those cartels, they want things done differently. They are the dogs of war, they go back and forth across the lines of your different countries without you even knowing, without them even getting out of bed. They're flexing muscle now, not as a show, but because they need to flex in order to grow. Television, internet, social media…you see people on that and hear about people in the news. Those people always getting reported on, always being quoted…you think those people are powerful? No…the people that have power are the ones that get dirty, the ones that don't care if anybody talks about them. The powerful people don't care if you know what they ate, what they wear…no, they just care that you fear them! You can sit behind your phone or computer and type all the things you want about everything and everybody and you may have a million people listening to you, but none of that is going to make a difference when someone shows up in the night, slits your throat and puts your head on a stick. Skin for skin! Yes, all that a man has he will give for his life[76]," Huerta snorted at me and walked over to a horse blanket in between a couple of ladies of ill repute, both of whom made eye contact with me and smiled that smile of come hither.

I was regaining my strength and my head was clearing. Huerta was smoking some sort of pipe out of 'Alice in Wonderland' and the vapor would obscure his face just before I could get a proper glimpse. The air had that dead, stale feel to it…not just in my nose and lungs, but on my skin. My comfort level began to wane and the unsettling nature of my surroundings washed over me. I stumbled a bit to my feet and then knelt down because my legs were in protest.

"Easy boy, you got a crawl before you walk," laughter erupted. I could have sworn that was Mr. Carlisle. I began to crawl on the dirt floor as the laughter grew louder. Dust was kicked in my face and voices mocked me. Someone stood over me from behind and grabbed my hair, forcing my head to face upwards.

"You're wasting your time, boy. Look around, you don't know where you're going or even where you are. We saved you. Remember…the crash, the people? You were exposed and we brought you back here to be saved," said Huerta. I weakly swatted at the hand and it let me go, dropping my face to the floor. I kept crawling. I didn't have a plan, but I knew I had to keep going. That's the best I could come up with at the time…keep going.

A boot came down in front of me, stopping my meager progression. "Look at your friends!" the voice boomed. My eyes were full of grit and goo, so I could barely make out anything. I lifted my head. I lost my breath as soon as I gained focus. I grew sick as the fear crawled up my back, engulfing my face with a hot rush. I couldn't believe it, but there in the corner, behind the smoke and darkness were two mounds lumped over each other. They were

---

[76] Job 2:4

people, with their limbs limp in defeat. Past the dried blood and dirt, I could see that the forms were Warden Robin Keller and Deputy Rudy Garza.

I gagged at the sight. There was slight movement, so they appeared to be alive, but what really got to me was the finality of the whole matter. They took the time to gather Rudy and Robin and me. We were not ignored…we were not too insignificant, and even more terrifying, we were all kept alive.

"Rudy?" I breathed. This was about as loud as I could project my voice. The head of one of the bodies moved at my call, but that was about as much as it could muster. I couldn't distinguish between Robin and Rudy as they were one limp mass. I began to crawl towards them when suddenly I felt myself being lifted off the ground by my clothes. I cried out in pain as my body ached with the sudden jerk. I was swiftly hurled on top of Robin and Rudy and made a part of that desperate pile of limbs and flesh.

I heard a moan underneath me upon my landing. I slid off to the side and found myself looking eye to eye with both of them. They both looked at me, void of expression, eyes of clouded glass and without blinking. If not for the slight movements and moans, I would have assumed they were dead. Their skin was dirty with mud, a mixture of dust, dirt and human fluids from them and others. Their faces, gender, skin color were indistinguishable from one another. The stench was of rot, which I assumed was my odor as well. We were one in the same…broken and lame.

Although our struggles and steps toward death seemed all consuming amongst the three of us, most of the occupants of the room appeared oblivious to our plight. Just moments before, I was a plaything, something to torment, but soon I was an afterthought. The laughter, smoke and dim lighting cradled us. While ours were moans of pain, the faint moan of pleasure from others seemed to seep into my ears. It was a contrast in mental states, yet everyone seemed just as dirty as us. Those that were smiling and blowing smoke looked as if they were covered in the same organic mud that the three of us had become. Why were they enjoying pleasures while we were dying? Maybe they were dying and just unaware of it.

"Deputy...Warden," I struggled again to try and coax some form of communication from them. I heard a responsive moan.

"We need to go," I muttered without regard to the lack of pragmatism. "We need to go, we need to go, we need to go…" I repeated this several times until I heard actual human communication.

"No," it was Robin. "No, we stay put, they will kill us, or…" she trailed off.

I switched my gaze to Deputy Rudy, who seemed to be roused a bit after hearing our exchange. He nodded to me and mustered the strength to agree with me, "We kill them on our way out."

I was startled. I didn't expect such a strong response from the Deputy. Especially given that he appeared almost dead. What did they do to him? What did they do to me? I couldn't be sure. I glanced around the room. There were no windows, but I did see a door. Nobody was guarding it, or us for that matter. I guess they didn't feel the need to be overly cautious. It wasn't as if we were in any shape to run anyway. There was enough people around to restrain us if need be, but it stills seemed strange that they wouldn't even bother tying us up. Although I really couldn't determine who these people were to begin with…were they part of a cartel, were they just partygoers or groupies of some sort or were they captives as well? Other than Huerta, there seemed to be no real structure, just a chaotic smoke filled room with one exit and nobody leaving.

The three of us began to quietly and weakly discuss our options. All I cared about was getting out of the room. It smelled of decay and it was menacing. The longer we were kept, the more likely something awful would happen to us as far as I was concerned. Rudy wanted out, but seemed resigned to his belief that we'd be killed anyway and really wanted to take some people down with him. None of us were thinking clearly, but Rudy was really interested in killing the bad guys. Robin, wanted nothing to do with either of our intentions. Whatever was done to her was so insidious that she was petrified. She refused to consider any act that appeared contrary to those that held us. She feared the consequences of our actions greater than what she already experienced. She feared the unknown. I for one believed they would do something awful and continue to do awful things to us in perpetuity no matter our actions. At least with my plan we had a shot at survival…of seeing the light of day again. Otherwise we were captives and we know for sure of nothing short of a horrid ending. We needed to come to our senses and escape from the snare of the devil![77]

For the most part, it was Rudy and me trying to convince Robin to leave with us. While Rudy's insistence on violence seemed ridiculous to me, it was an argument for another time. We needed to convince Robin to come with us or we would need to address the possibility of abandonment. From my perspective, this was the moment to leave, when we were perceived as weak, when nobody was paying attention. They could see it in my eyes and I could feel them sensing the urgency.

I tensed my muscles a bit, just to see if they worked. I was not going to wait for things to happen to me, I needed out. I looked at Rudy and he gave me a slight nod. He was ready. Robin just looked at us, but I thought she might follow if we took the initiative. I tried to lick my

---

[77] 2 Tim. 2:26

lips, but there was no moisture in my mouth. My lips were cracked and caked with grit. I tensed again, trying to get the adrenaline going before making my break. I accepted that this was a live or die moment.

I began to spring up, but was impeded by a sharp and forceful pain in my back. Rudy and Robin turned from me quickly. I felt the end of a cane or walking stick being jabbed into me with the full weight of a man. A voice from behind bellowed, "I think it's cage time for these three!" Laughter and cheers rose up in response. "They look like they've got the itch. They haven't quite learned that it's best to submit to Huerta!" the voice boomed as confirming murmurs swirled about with the smoke.

"You've got to go along and get along my friends. It's a new life for you now. You understand? Or really, it's your old life…you just haven't realized it yet. We'll talk later after you calm down in the cage. It will all be clear by then. Just know…you're going nowhere!" Huerta jabbed me again with his stick and chuckled to himself. Then I felt several hands grab and drag me along the dirt floor along with the others. I pawed at the ground be it was just crumbling dirt, nothing to grab hold.

We were pulled to the center of the room into a small rusty cage, thrown in and the door slammed behind us. We had no walls, we were exposed to all, but behind bars. They watched us, like we were some macabre centerpiece for the room.

"Lights out!" boomed Huerta. Everything went black.

Chapter 10 - The Darkness.

It was completely dark. I could feel the presence of others throughout the room. I could hear the snickering, the breathing, the cursing and murmuring. The lights were out, but we were not alone. I kept my arm in constant contact with either Rudy or Robin, it was impossible to decipher who was who within the cage. We dared not speak, we just listened. When in danger and blinded, one must listen and not provoke. I could hear the sound of chains being moved about and a metal coming into contact, like some sort of crank being operated.

Suddenly, I felt the bottom of the cage being lifted as my weight pressed down upon the bars. There was a squeeze on my arm from one of my fellow captives as we were raised. We were probably suspended no more than four feet off the ground, but I wouldn't know for sure. Now I could hear the snickering and murmuring from all directions, including beneath me. It was as if we were floating in ocean at night, amongst the sharks with no protection in any direction. Every few moments I would feel a tug from below or a poke with a stick or some other sharp object. It would come from on top, below, behind, in front or from the sides. There was no timing pattern to the harassment, no rhythm, no rhyme, no reason. Each time that I caught my breath and settled I would get jabbed by a stick or my skin pinched by some dirty fingers that snaked through the bars. On occasion I'd feel a poke from something sharp like a knife and I could feel the blood drip. These were painful attacks, horrifying in fact, but not enough to kill, just enough to torture.

I don't know how long this ordeal lasted, as time and space seemed irrelevant. These people were blinded in mind as in sight.[78] For the most part I was paranoid, on edge, asking myself when the next poke, pinch or even bite would occur. It was maddening. The biting was

---

[78] 2 Cor. 4:4

most disturbing because of the intimacy. To bite in between the bars of a cage requires effort and closeness to the victim. I imagined that the perpetrators even sustained a level of pain themselves as their mouths were pressed against the rusty metal and I would twitch and swat back at these attacks. When one goes through something that is terrifying, one's body and mind begin to do things that otherwise would never be experienced. I began to look forward to the less painful experiences, which in normal everyday life, I would not tolerate. I was grateful for a pinch or a jab from a stick or when someone decided to swing the cage about. I didn't think of my family or my life in general. There were no big picture worries. All focus was on avoiding the biting or anything that involved blood.

This torture became normalized quickly and I adjusted my mental and physical state to handle them. When the aggression took place, it hurt physically, but there was a mental relief because the anticipation was over. The torture was twisted in the waiting…the anticipation of it all. The cycle of pain would restart every few moments and no relief seemed to be in sight. As demoralizing as the situation was, it soon would become much worse.

The room suddenly got real quiet, then the murmuring began again and the snickering was more intense. Something really entertaining to these creatures must have been in the midst. I saw a small orange glowing orb slightly below me, or was it in the distance? It was pitch black, so there was no perspective of how far away anything was especially if it emitted any light. I watched and didn't see it move. Occasionally something passed in front of the orb, blocking out the light for a moment. Then it began. A small glowing piece lifted from the orb and began to move about, suspended at eye level. It moved swiftly, the murmuring and giggling grew more intense. I could sense the heat from the glowing tip, it disappeared quickly underneath us and I heard Robin scream in such a way that I've never heard before. I heard the searing, the laughter and the light was no more. Then another glowing piece appeared, suspended in air, disappeared and I felt Rudy squeeze my arm as he screamed in agony. I smelled the burning flesh.

Then came mine…I could not make a sound. My mind left and I prayed for death. I didn't feel anything until moments later when the pain on my thigh was so bad that it radiated up to my ear. I didn't dare touch the burn, I didn't want to know. I could barely breathe. I didn't want to anticipate anything else, I just wanted it to be finished. I hoped that someone would hit me in the head to knock me out, but nothing of the sorts happened. I heard Huerta's voice again yell, "Lights out I said!"

Everything went silent again other than the violent hissing from the water being poured on whatever coals were used to heat the burning pikes. Huerta yelled again, "Get some sleep, we've got a lot to discuss!" It was his own twisted slumber party.

I did not sleep. If I did sleep it was of little use. The line between consciousness and unconsciousness had been blurred since the moment things went awry for me…since the moment I met Mr. Carlisle for what seemed so long ago. Was it years ago or just a few days? Time and space have little meaning when suspended in darkness. Every so often the cage was pushed or pulled to cause us to sway, but besides that, we were left alone. However, as a victim, such technicalities gave little comfort. I, as I'm sure my fellow captives, spent whatever time was meant for sleep anticipating the next torture or trying to decipher whether a tormentor was a few inches from my face or just my eyes playing tricks on me due to the room being devoid of any light. Your eyes and mind can fool you, especially when there are shadows, but when your entire world is a shadow, the monsters inside your consciousness come forth and dance in front of you without any mercy. There were points, throughout what I presume was night, where I was close to screaming in terror, but the terror of drawing attention outweighed the terror for the sake of terror.

Many people spend a portion of their lives trying to find themselves. It's a waste of time and a task that lacks nobility. While unknown to me as I swung in a nightmare abyss, I would determine later that finding oneself is, by its own admission, both selfish and ridiculous. To find oneself is egotistical. It is a quest of elevated self-importance. You are the center of the universe. You are not trying to find a cure for an ailment, find a missing child, find peace or love. No, you are trying to find yourself, others be damned. It's a sad endeavor, really.

A strange aunt of mine had a bird. She loved this obnoxious bird. It might have been a parakeet. It was not an ugly bird by any means, but it could not smile or hug you or tell you it was there for you. The bird's song was terrible. It was a bit colorful, which was nice. The bird seemed to be healthy. Its cage was disgusting though, and it often flung food all about the area beyond the cage. I could not imagine a scenario that would justify paying any sum of money for this bird, but my aunt viewed it as priceless. One of the bird's favorite pastimes was to look at itself in the mirror. It thought that its reflection was that of another bird. It spent countless hours watching, biting and communicating with this reflection and for absolutely no reason. It was interacting with itself the entire time. That bird spent half its life seeking the companionship of another bird when all it had was its reflection. It was looking for someone else, but was stuck with itself. These people that look for themselves…they're really looking for someone else. They don't like the reflection. The reflection is not good enough; they need something more, something better. I didn't realize it at the time, but when you lose your dignity, physical strength and mental capacity…when you live in fear of dying…of being tortured…when you are floating in darkness…you stop seeking yourself and you seek something else. That reflection becomes just a reflection and nothing more. You don't need to find yourself, because you were there the entire time. This was you stripped down to your pure reptilian self. In a sense, torture was a form of freedom.

As we floated in the darkness I heard for the first time some noise from Robin other than the reactionary sounds of torture. She was sobbing. I was surprised. I couldn't muster any emotion in the state I was either in physically or mentally. I was exhausted and thought death was the most sensible relief. Yet Robin somehow remained human enough to cry… quietly, seemingly to herself. I even heard her whispering some things, "I deserve this," she would whisper. "I was wrong, so wrong to do it," she continued. Robin repeated these things and sobbed again and again. She kept confessing some unnamed wrongdoings, sins of some nature, all vague and almost generic. She was just bad or did something wrong. Over and over this went on until eventually Robin began to raise her voice.

"I'm bad! I'm wrong! I deserve this!" Robin shouted again and again. Rudy and I grabbed her and tried to settle her down for we both feared drawing attention, but she continued almost fueled by our attempt to stifle her.

"I'm bad! I'm wrong! I deserve this!" she shouted.

"I'm bad! I'm wrong! I deserve this!" louder and louder she repeated. She began to rock back and forth in a state of delirium. The murmuring from the dark began to grow. It was a call and response. Robin shouted, then the murmurs reacted. My heart was beating faster, my adrenaline raised. I shouted back words of comfort, "You're not bad. You are good. You do not deserve this." Rudy would say the same things and Robin would just shout "no" and continue her rants. Hands were grabbing the cage, shaking and swinging it in response. Things were getting out of control and evil presence in the room was feeding off of it.

Robin shouted louder, Rudy and I shouted back and the people in the dark began whooping and screaming in delight, spinning our cage and swinging it back and forth. They grabbed at us and poked while shrieking in delight. It was chaos.

"Enough!" boomed the voice as a torch entered the darkness. Lamps and candles began to light as the room slowly showed itself. Huerta stood by the cage and surveyed his world. Torch in hand, Huerta walked a few feet in front of us and planted the torch into the ground, casting the irregular flickering light on our faces like a Rorschach Test. Everyone, including Robin, went silent.

Huerta walked back and forth between us and the dirty smirking faces surrounding us. He paused and turned, looking us over as if he was choosing one of us for an entree. He wasn't quite as filthy as his subjects, but he wasn't clean either. He wasn't ethnically distinctive, nor was his size striking in any manner. Other than his booming voice and sense of command, I found nothing outwardly significant about this strange and intimidating being. There were no tattoos, no scars, nothing unique about his hair, but he did have the appearance of control. Most of all, I could taste something menacing, something evil when he appeared. No matter what he looked like or how he acted, I felt the evil aura about him.

However physically unremarkable Huerta appeared in my eyes, he seemed like a god to those troll-like people mulling about in that cavern. They did what he asked or I should say, they reacted to him, like roaches scurrying about when the light switch was thrown. These people with their dirty faces, smiling and watching…they seemed more like animals to be corralled and herded along rather than any army to be commanded. There didn't appear to be any sort of rank and file, just a crowd being lead in one direction or another by Huerta's voice or just them moving out of his way while he walked about.

The followers themselves were nothing like anything I'd noticed before. They were disgusting, filthy creatures, dead behind the eyes with a flash every now and then when whipped into a frenzy as if they had a taste for flesh. They fed off of stimuli, reacting when excitement was sensed, out of control unless corralled by Huerta. It was controlled chaos. Huerta allowed the frenzy until it infringed on his will. When his followers were getting too unruly for him, Huerta would shout and wave his hands and they would scatter about, then congregate around him again when he stopped his threats. He really just herded them along.

Huerta stared at us a bit, then smirked to himself and began his speech, "You are tired, hungry, weak and broken. I will feed you and keep you safe. You are free to come and go as you please, but I own you. Do you understand? That mark we put on your leg, is my brand. Is not this a brand plucked from the fire?[79] I own you. You can leave if you like, but that desert will kill you, that cartel will kill you or my people will kill you. I'm not going to tell them to get you, but they will, because that's what they do and I'll do nothing to stop them." The dirty followers giggled and muttered excitedly at this prospect.

"Let me tell you something," Huerta continued, shaking his head as he spoke, "...let me tell you, if the cartel gets you, they will torture you, if the desert gets you, it will torture you, and you can damn sure bet that if my people get you...oh, you wish it would be just torture." The room erupted in howls of approval. Huerta walked by and swung the cage. The movement of the cage alone caused another uproar of excitement in the room. Smoke billowed about as he smiled, allowing his people to delight with it all for a bit before he continued.

"When it has gone out of you, it passes through waterless places seeking rest, but finds none.[80] Gone are the days of just killing witnesses or adversaries. I don't do that anymore and

---

[79] Zech. 3:2
[80] Mat. 12:43

neither do the cartels or any other organization for that matter. No, we see what the rest of the world is doing. We've watched those that claim to be sons of Ismail, chopping off heads, lighting heathens on fire, putting them in cages. It's effective. I don't want to kill you, I want to convert you. We just don't pretend that God is involved like they do. You can make up any excuse you want, but they're just a gang of criminals like us, making money, stealing, raping. We're just honest about it. There is no god, period. If there was, why are you here and why are those folks chopping off heads in his name? Would you let someone kill children in your name? Huh? I don't think you would and God still calls you a sinner. If you, a sinner, wouldn't let someone kill a child in your name, then why would God, who is perfect? How can someone who is perfect, all powerful and all-knowing allow that to happen? I know why and you know why…because he isn't there. He's not there, he's not here, he's not anywhere. We all can be gods if we so desire and right now… I am your god," Huerta said. He looked at us closely, making sure we understood.

"You become one of us. You already are anyway. I heard your companion crying, she knows she's no better than the rest of us. Neither are you two, don't act like you're any better than her either. I know what you've done. You're already one of us. I don't really make anybody do anything, I just facilitate. I run the river, you help me run the river if you want protection. I've got an understanding with the real bad guys. I make sure they are able to get what they need back and forth and they give me a taste and leave me alone. That's the deal and that's why it's my river. Sometimes it's about opportunity. I don't care about you folks, but the cartel does. I knew they would be very interested in me getting ahold of you three. Consider yourself lucky, they used the old ways on the others that knew too much. I'm keeping you alive. It's not bad. You want to run a scheme somewhere, take a bit off the top, you go right ahead.

You just make sure that you give me what is mine. You see? It all works. Now, we may lose a person here or there, but you don't have to worry about your job, family, or to any regulations. This is an underground economy. There are no borders, no countries. I've got American friends coming back and forth with the Mexicans, Hondurans, Salvadorans and so on. Hell, before he died, I was working with a Nazi that moved down here after World War Two! That guy could get things done and at his age! None of us care about governments, counties, or borders. I don't care about truth, I have nothing to do with truth.[81] We do what we want. You see? So…it's up to you. You stay with us and you make of it what you want, or you leave and see what happens to you. Now…I've got business to attend," and with that Huerta promptly turned and pushed open a wooden door. The light poured in, blinding me. Now I knew there was a way out.

Huerta stuck his head back through the door and said, "That cage…that cage is not locked," and he disappeared again.

We swung in that cage, stunned by what Huerta just said. The cage was unlocked. I didn't even see a lock in the first place. Who would think to look? Kidnappers put us in a cage with no lock? How could I have been so stupid? Huerta was counting on us not running or did he not care? I thought that maybe he was right. If we left, he would just tell the cartel that we left and they'd come and kill us. His animals that made up his followers would probably get to us first and use us as chew toys. In my mind, there was no choice about what to do. I had to escape. If I stayed, the outcome was predetermined. My family would be without me and in danger. I would be killed, tortured or become one of these creatures surrounding Huerta. There was no alternative. I may fail and horrible things may happen to me, but I needed a chance.

---

[81] John 8:44

Staying put was no solution. The hope was that the others would go with me. I was hurt, tired and hungry and I had no idea what extent of injuries Rudy and Robin had undertaken.

"We've got to go," I said to Rudy and Robin. They turned and looked at me. Rudy nodded sternly.

"Do you think you can walk?" I asked.

"I will. Scratched, bruises, cuts and the like. My problem is that it's going to have to be adrenaline that gets me out. Then how much energy are we going to have once we leave? If that guy is right and we're in desert or scrub, we won't last long," said Rudy.

"Yeah…but I think I'd rather die out there than in here with these guys," I responded. Rudy nodded in agreement. Robin just stared. She didn't pay any attention to what was said. She just stared glassy eyed like a fish left out of the water too long, just gasping and gradually fading away…a live, vibrant active being from another world suddenly drying out, losing color and transforming into another form, lifeless, but a new creation nonetheless.

"Robin…Robin, you have to talk to us. Robin, we need you on board," I reached over and held her arm, hoping that human contact, without evil intention, could snap her back into our world. She slowly turned her head towards me. Robin's eyes still glassy and clouded. She didn't know what she was seeing when she looked at me. I could have been a wall or just the air as far as she knew.

"Robin, Deputy Garza and I are going to leave. You've got to come with us. If you stay, there's no hope for you. We've got to try and leave." She shook her head slowly back and forth and then it grew faster.

"No! No...no," Robin snapped at me. Her eyes now beginning to focus in on my face. Rudy breathed heavy in frustration and we both tried to calm her. She kept saying "no" over and over, her eyes darting around the room. The followers began to get excited again.

"Robin...if we don't leave, they're going to tear you apart. Don't you see it? Look at them," pleaded Deputy Garza as he squeezed her arm, trying to convince her.

"No! I don't want to leave. They'll kill us out there. If I stay, I might be able to leave later, when it's safer...it's safer in here," said Robin. She was breathing hard. I could tell that she didn't want us to leave, but she knew we would. She was panicking. She didn't' want to leave. She was stuck and she knew it.

"Martin! They're going to the lights!" Deputy Garza shouted. I looked up and saw the people hopping about, becoming more and more excitable. I saw one licking his lips at me from up against the wall. Then one of the lights went out. They were making it dark again.

"We've got to go now!" shouted Deputy Garza. I nodded.

"Robin! Now! We're leaving now! They're going to do something if we don't go!" I was pleading with her, but she shook her head. Another light went out and it was getting darker.

"Let's open the cage," said Deputy Garza as he pushed the top open. The room became noisy with screeches of glee.

"Robin, they're coming!" I screamed.

She didn't look up, but shouted, "Leave me alone, I will stay here and serve him. It's better than dying out there![82]"

Another light went out, there was one left. "Remember where the door is. It's about to go dark!" shouted Garza. I could see them closing in on us, just a few feet away and then it went

---

[82] Ex. 14:12

pitch black again. The air was filled with shrieking as we began our scramble. Their dirty hands were grasping for me under the cage. Deputy Garza kicked me in the head as he jumped out. I heard yells and grunts as he must have been fighting through the group towards the door. The cage was swinging and Robin was being slung back and forth, knocking me about until I was able to grab the sides of the exit. With all my strength I hoisted myself out and fell face first onto the dirt floor and some feet.

I was immediately being grabbed at from all sides. Completely blind I began to thrash about as I was being swarmed by these terrible beings. I still had a sense of where the door was located and began to push forward while fighting off the beings attacking me. One got ahold of my ear and hair and I could feel a tearing of skin and hair. I continued to push and punch, keeping my face pointing down to avoid losing an eye.

I was losing strength and hope began to fade. I had no perception of distance, so I wasn't sure if I'd made any progress at all. The more I was grabbed and pulled, the further back I began to feel. I needed some way of knowing where I was in comparison to the door. It was like the nightmare I'd always had as a child. The one where something was chasing me, but I couldn't move or scream. I was living my nightmare out in real time.

Then a crack of light appeared. There it was! This was all I needed. I could see Deputy Garza's figure as he threw open the door. Bodies went flying as he punched and pushed at the captors. The sunlight was blinding, but glorious. I rammed my way through on nothing but my lifeless blood pumping through my body.

"Let's go!" screamed Deputy Garza as I pushed my way to him. I could hear what I thought was Robin screaming, but I didn't stop or pay it much attention. Once I caught up to him we ran. He a couple yards ahead of me, neither one of us looking back. We ran and ran, past scrub and a few abandoned cars scattered about. It was just rocky desert in front of us, just a horizon, but we ran. For a good half an hour we ran without stopping, my lungs burned with the dust and heat and the agony of strain. All I heard was my footsteps banging on the ground and the wheezing of my lungs as I ran from the horrors behind me.

Chapter 11 – The Desert.

Deputy Garza finally glanced back. He did it again, this time his eyes looked confused. Then he just stopped. I was bewildered until I turned around. Nobody seemed to be following us.

"We must have jogged at least three miles," Deputy Garza said in confusion, "where the hell are they?" I looked around and saw didn't see anybody in any direction. I couldn't even see a building where we being held. It was as if the whole thing was a mirage. Deputy Garza had a look of bewilderment on his face, which I'm sure matched mine.

"I don't see the place. Where did we come from?" I asked.

"I don't know. There were stairs leading out of the room and after the first door, I pushed open a pair of raggedy double doors, like for a cellar. I think we might have been underground," said Deputy Garza. This made sense. This Huerta guy must have literally been operating underground. I don't recall seeing any guards or even any guns for that matter. If the cage wasn't locked then the doors probably weren't either. He was just out of sight.

"Rudy, I didn't see anybody guarding us or the door, did you?"

"No. This guy doesn't operate the same as the others. Those cartels, they've got guard posts, men with machine guns at gates, in towers, cameras, razor wire and walls. This guy…I don't remember seeing anybody with a gun. It was crazy. The cartels have some order. There are middle men, rank and file from the top down. This Huerta, it was just him and a bunch of lunatics. No locks, no buildings, no guards, no right hand men, no walls, no guns. I've never heard of this type of thing."

I thought about Huerta, how his appearance was nothing special, there was no jewelry, no fast cars, the women were disgusting, no mansion...he shattered all my criminal stereotypes. What was his motivation? It was always money wasn't it?

"He's underground. I bet he has a bunch of spaces dug out. If they're not connected, then it's got to be harder to find right? Say you find one of these dens of his, you don't know how many more there are out there and who or what he has in them. They could all be right there together or they could each be a mile apart. You could kick in the door of one, but he might have ten others sitting out there with resources, victims, and people that you didn't find. Think about it, if they were all connected with tunnels or something, if you were law enforcement, all you need to do is find one and you've found them all. This way...this way means finding one gives you only a small fraction of the big picture," it was coming together for me and I could see Deputy Garza was working on it in his mind as well.

"I bet he has these in Texas! You heard him. He doesn't care about borders. He's not some sort of drug producer or seller like the cartels, he's a facilitator. He found a niche and owns it. The cartels don't mess with him because he provides them with services. Think about it, he can hide their men on both sides of the borders, kidnap people, store drugs, migrants...I mean it's endless if you think about it. He had no accent, did you catch that?" Deputy Garza was getting excited as he pieced everything together.

"I assumed he was Mexican, but I couldn't hear an accent either. Where is this guy from? He's got to be American, right?" I asked.

"He's a myth in law enforcement. We've heard of him, but none of us thought he was an actual guy. Even if we did think he was real, the stories didn't seem to be true and probably weren't. It was all sorts of super human stories. Did you notice that he wasn't a big guy or

148

anything? He was pretty average all the way around. The stories about him were just too fantastic to believe. How big he was or strong, missing an eye…but seeing him, nobody would suspect this guy of being Huerta," said Deputy Garza.

"If people barely see him and he's got spots all over the place, I bet stories just start cropping up. Why is he doing this though? He's not posting pictures of his house, car, women, cash or anything. The place was grotesque. Nobody sane would want to live in these little underground rooms. It smelled like it was rotting," I remarked.

Deputy Garza shook his head. It didn't make sense to him either. It's all about perspective really. Maybe Huerta would rather be a god of filth than no god at all. I knew people like that. They'd rather be under the radar, shifty, flexible and be a master of their own domain than succumb to a traditional way of life. It was also smart…the less glamorous one's lifestyle, the less attention it received. He let the cartels be the target of gang wars and law enforcement, while he ran much of the show behind the scenes. The shelf life of a higher up in a cartel was about the same as ice-cream dropped on a sidewalk. Huerta on the other hand, his shelf life was whatever he decided. What he gave up in gauche opulence, he made up for in longevity.

"You know, guys like that…the Manson types that just talk and bring in folks, they're responsible for murders, drugs, theft, whatever… but they never do it themselves. They don't have to, you know, they have these people doing all their dirty work for him. I've seen this stuff before, not this size though. You know, it's the lawless one, they come in with an appearance of power and false signs and wonders.[83] How do normal, smart people fall for this? I had a case once, love triangle type thing. This woman, not attractive, not rich, nothing special about her. In

---

[83] 2 Thes. 2:9

fact, she was just flat out rotten from what I remember. You and I might look at her and ignore her, but these men...these men would do anything for her. She had two guys on the side and convinced both of them to kill her husband, and they did. Just like that, just because she asked. I couldn't believe it. What was it about her that made these guys commit murder? She rolled over on them too, as soon as they got caught, she blamed them and tried to get away with it. We knew better and so did the jury, but it was a light sentence because she really didn't do much. She didn't pay the guys, she didn't physically kill her husband. She just asked her two lovers to kill him, that's it. Even in jail those men wouldn't turn on her. It was the craziest thing. What is it about these people that can convince other folks to jut commit murder?" Deputy Garza asked.

I shrugged my shoulders. I had no clue. Deputy Garza continued, "Well I thought about it for some time and I think I figured it out. She wasn't charismatic, she wasn't pretty and she wasn't nice. So did she have something these guys wanted? Nope. I'll tell you what it was, it has nothing to do with her appearance, speaking ability or any type of lifestyle for these guys. This lady was just good at finding suckers. That's it. You and I wouldn't fall for her, but these guys...they couldn't see her for what she was. For some reason, they were the type that would keep falling for ladies like her, over and over again. Men and women both fall for these type of people. They crave someone telling them what to do, how to think and so forth. These guys were susceptible and she was good at spotting people like that and clinging tightly to them. This Huerta, he draws lost souls and he uses them to do his will. I guess they can be outwitted by him if they are ignorant of his designs.[84] He tempts in the wilderness.[85]"

We rested for a bit, still looking back to where we thought the hideout was located. Neither one of us could see anything. I was starting to question if any of it was real until the

---

[84] 2 Cor. 2:11
[85] Matt. 4:1

searing of Huerta's brand radiated back through my leg. They branded me right through my pants. I could see a hole burned through Deputy Garza's as well. My fear had now subsided enough to where I was feeling all of my wounds and ailments. Between the car wreck, kidnapping and torture, my body was broken. I couldn't remember the last time I ate or drank anything. From the looks of it Deputy Garza was in no better shape.

"Did you get into a car wreck?" I asked Garza. He nodded.

"Me too," I said. Deputy Garza nodded again. He didn't seem surprised. I wasn't either. It was how they operated.

I was weak and everything hurt. I sat down and scanned the horizon. It looked like desert or scrub country in all directions. I needed water, I needed food and I needed rest. We both did.

"We need to find food, water and a place to rest," I said to Garza.

"Yep, we need to get moving," he replied. Garza got up looked up at the sun and started walking. I followed, asking him for clarification as to why we were going that particular direction.

"North, to the border. We've got no money or anything, so we need to get home," said Garza, his voice was labored.

"What about the local police or whatever law enforcement they have around here?"

"Nope, they'll give us back to Huerta or the cartel will have them kill us. We'll likely be killed at the border anyway, probably by one of our border guards or someone I know in the sheriff's department. We've got better odds than going to the locals though," said Garza.

Deputy Garza fancied himself a bit of a survivalist. I had no idea the extent of his survival knowledge, though it seemed suspect. He was in just as bad shape as me and was just as desperate to get home as he knew our time was short. He began walking in what I considered an arbitrary direction. He claimed it was north. The pace was brisk, but steady. We needed to get as far away from Huerta as possible, yet we both knew our energy reserves were limited.

My head was on a swivel, constantly scanning the scrub and horizon for enemies. I would look back on occasion as well, but we were alone. There was not a cloud in the sky and the heat was merciless. I didn't need to mention that to Garza. When you're with someone who is suffering the same as you, verbal communication is only necessary to send and receive useful information, for action purposes. Nobody needs to know how each other feels or that life is difficult for everyone's lives are difficult at that particular point in time. We were walking and scanning the area for anything that could help us stay alive. Deputy Garza picked up an old tin can lid that someone must have thrown out twenty years before. I didn't know why he picked it up, but in hard times you tend to grab things and assume you can use them down the road.

After some time, my physical pain and suffering supplanted my fear of Huerta's people. I remember seeing those nature shows every now and then on television where a group of zebras want to drink at a watering hole. The watering hole is drying up and there are twenty giant crocodiles just lying in wait. All the animals see the crocodiles, yet the zebras go forth to drink. Everyone knows that a zebra will die, and yet their thirst is so desperate that it overwhelms their fear of being eaten alive. They drink anyway and the crocodiles attack, killing a zebra while the others run away. All for a sip of dirty water. That sip was worth it.

My tongue was swelled by this point and I would not have been able to speak if willing. I could see it in Deputy Garza's eyes as well. My lips were covered in dust, but I had no saliva to remove it, nor did I want to because the dust felt better than the air. My lungs burned with each breath and I felt as if very little sweat was left to push out of my skin. Our pace slowed after an hour and we needed to have some moisture soon. We were wandering aimlessly in the land; the wilderness had shut us in.[86]

We saw a clump of cacti off to the right and made our way towards it. The hope was to get some sort of hydration from the cacti. I sat down and Deputy Garza used the tin can top that he'd picked up earlier to start cutting a hole into a cactus. It was as tall as we were and thick enough for Deputy Garza to hand me the top halfway through. I finished it up and we took turns using our hands as ladles inside the cactus. It wasn't much, but it felt like a rejuvenation. A little goes a long way when you have nothing. We rested in the tiny amount of shade the cacti provided. This looked like the only bit of shelter for miles.

Deputy Garza was looking at me, I could tell by his expression that I appeared like I was not long for the world. He looked the same. After we rested a bit, Deputy Garza spoke up, "I don't think we can make it to another spot like this today, not during the day. We need to rest and travel at night. Maybe some lizards or bugs will show up when the sun starts going down, we can eat some of them. We need something or we won't make it. We've got nothing to cook with, so we'll just eat them raw. Just eat what you can catch." It was a good theory, I wasn't sure it could be put to practice though. It didn't matter, we couldn't go any further anyway. I didn't know how long we were walking, but it was most of the day. After what we went through, we wouldn't make it even a few more feet.

I nodded and put my shirt over my head and fell asleep. Deputy Garza did the same. I would wake up every once and awhile thinking someone was standing over me, but when I looked around, there wasn't a living soul in any direction other than Garza. I would see that the shadow had moved and I'd scoot over to the shadow and go back asleep. It felt like I slept for

---

[86] Ex. 14:3

hours, but I'm sure it was just a few minutes at a time. Eventually the sun started to angle down and I began to regain a bit of energy as the temperature cooled. Deputy Garza began to stir as well.

Once the sun fell beyond the horizon, we both stood up and began to look for things to eat. Nothing appeared. I just started scraping the inside of the cactus and ate that. Deputy Garza did as well. It probably offered nothing of substance, but it was enough to give us the confidence to walk again, which we did.

Walking in the cool of the night with a bit of substance in our stomachs was much more productive than our daytime walk. Deputy Garza seemed to think he was taking us in the right direction although he never fully told me how he came to such a conclusion. He would occasionally look up at the moon or the stars and nod to himself as if they were providing him with the appropriate guidance. This was all plausible of course as people had been using the stars and other naturally occurring elements to chart their paths for thousands of years. My skepticism was related to a modern man using these same methods. What was the likelihood that a sheriff's deputy just so happened to know how to chart a course using the stars? What was the likelihood that this man living in the Rio Grande Valley of Texas had also been a sailor? Not only are the odds quite long that such a man even existed, but also happened to be paired up with me and lost in the desert lands of Mexico after we were kidnapped? No, I wasn't confident in his abilities, but I didn't have any other options.

Mexico…how did I even know we were in Mexico? I've been on both sides of the river and if there weren't signs or people, I wouldn't know the difference. What if we had been captive in Texas this whole time? Could we have been in another country all together? I was unconscious, but for how long? Were we in El Salvador or Honduras? Not with this landscape.

154

Although how would I really know? We were either in the U.S. or Mexico. How far south we were was a different question. I could have been in Texas this whole time. Huerta could have these underground dens all over the place.

"Rudy...which direction are we going again?" I asked.

"North," he replied. He was puzzled by the question.

"Why?"

"Because we're going home."

"How do you know we're in Mexico?"

Deputy Garza stopped and stared at me for a bit. He shook his head and looked around. He walked over to me, stood for a second then asked, "Well where the hell else would we be?"

"I don't know...Texas. Who knows, maybe New Mexico or Arizona," I replied.

"Why would we be in Arizona?" Deputy Garza shouted. He was irritated.

"I don't know. That's the thing...why do you think we're in Mexico?"

"Where else would we be?"

"They knocked me out. Didn't they do the same with you?" I asked. Deputy Garza nodded. "Well...if we're in Mexico, I can't tell the difference between the terrain here or in Texas. It all looks the same to me. There's no shops or signs or people. Those people that were around us underground...I couldn't tell where they were from. Huerta was speaking English and those animals weren't talking at all really. They operated underground, who's to say they weren't underground in Texas? Same with the cartels, they're getting bolder and bolder right? I mean, none of these people care about a border or boundaries. Remember a few years ago when they threatened to kill the mayor of El Paso? I've always assumed that they move stuff over to one side or the other, but primarily stay in their own country, but I don't know if that's the case anymore do you? Huerta didn't seem to care about any of that stuff one way or the other."

Deputy Garza spit in the dirt, squinted at the stars and said, "I'm going north. I don't care where we are. It doesn't matter. If we're in Texas or Mexico I'm going north. You know why? Because it doesn't matter! If we're in Mexico, we're going north to get to the border. If we're in Texas, we're going north to get the hell away from the border! Got it?" I nodded. He quickly turned and started walking again.

Deputy Garza began to lecture me without bothering to look back at me, "You wasted too much time with that garbage! It wouldn't have changed the direction we are going either way! Waste of time! Who cares where we are? Wherever we are, we need to go away from it!"

He was right, ultimately. I still would have liked to have known where we were, just for my own edification. It didn't matter where we were, it mattered where we were going. In our particular journey we were going away from where we were. We needed to flee and survive the process of fleeing. We didn't know where we were, but we knew we couldn't be there. That was the situation for a lot of people in life. They don't know where they are, but they knew they shouldn't be there. The only safe direction we knew to go was north. We didn't know exactly the ultimate destination, but we knew north was best. When under duress and in a life and death situation, the specific details of things are ignored because they are irrelevant. That was the entirety of Deputy Garza's point. We were dying from the elements or potentially being pursed, with intent of death and any details involving our ultimate geographic location were irrelevant.

The real trick is not that we needed to flee and go north, the two of us could not disagree about that; it's whether or not Deputy Garza was actually leading us north. The problem was that I had no alternative. I had no knowledge of navigation or any sense of direction of where we were. This meant that any other direction I chose to go besides that of Deputy Garza was going to be chosen at random. I had no frame of reference other than observing Deputy Garza staring up at the sky and the fact that he did provide us with the innards of a cactus, which is more than I'd provided. So, I had no choice. I had to follow him.

The night was cool and the pace was brisk. I felt like I had been run over by a truck, but with my thirst and hunger temporarily quenched and with the sun out of the picture, I was walking along better than before. Fear played a great role in this uptick in energy as well. I could see that Deputy Garza was experiencing a similar rejuvenation of sorts. It was temporary of course, but we needed it. Fear comes back when hunger, thirst and exhaustion subside. Fear requires energy and hope. When you're hopeless, there's nothing to fear. Hopelessness is a source of freedom from fear. Fear was a gift for the strong and healthy.

Our fears would eventually become a self-fulfilling prophecy, as we would discover that we were not alone. We had been walking throughout the night, stopping only to cut open another cactus. Eventually, the landscape began to change to more of a scrub terrain. Still dry, dirty and more or less barren, but the scrub brush began to pop up around us, like miniature trees. Eventually, these scrubby bushes turned into short cedar trees here and there. With a moonlit night, light and shadows emerged with the scrub trees, causing me to see things that may not actually be there.

For the most part, my head was down, looking at Deputy Garza's feet. I would glance up once and awhile and swear I would see something duck behind the scrub. This happened on several occasions. I was almost afraid to mention anything to Deputy Garza, based on old childhood fears. You are in your room at night, it's dark and you're scared. You think you hear something down the hall, so you pull the sheets over your head and stay completely still and quiet. As if this would ward off the monster outside your door. Instincts are ingrained in the back of your mind and are often wrong, contrary to what some might say. Pull the sheets over your head does nothing but keep you from seeing the monster. I was afraid to speak up to Deputy Garza because I thought for some reason it would cause an attack. If something were following us, speaking up would have little effect on what the monsters would do. It didn't matter. I breathed slowly and only searched for the beings with my peripheral vision, always keeping my eyes pointed at Deputy Garza's shoes. Maybe if they thought I was unaware, I could have caught them off guard. That thought lingered a bit, and was as nonsensical as the other rationales I created for my silence.

At some point, the monsters will make an appearance, they always do. It's in their nature to be monstrous, that's why they're called monsters. I tried to ignore my doubts and press on, concentrating on Deputy Garza's feet again, but then it became undeniable. I heard movement on the ground behind me to my right. I turned quickly, but couldn't make out anything. There was something there this time. I had no idea if it were human or animal. I just knew something was with us.

"There's something out there," I said to Deputy Garza.

"Keep going," he answered.

When I stopped, I heard nothing, but as soon as I moved I could hear footsteps behind me. This went on for some time, stopping and starting, footsteps and silence. My hope was that it was an animal. However irrational, I preferred a dangerous animal over a dangerous human. I always felt like there was at least a chance that I would be able to outsmart the animal. As far as humans are concerned, it always seemed to me that victory went to the most sociopathic or the person who cared the least about consequences.

We walked for several moments until I finally received the visual confirmation that I dreaded. Heads began to peek out from behind the trees and scrub. They would pop up, giggle and fall back. They were scattered about all around us. They would peek out and then hide as soon as we would make our way even with them. I knew Deputy Garza saw them. Neither of us needed to say anything. We knew we were in trouble. We knew these were Huerta's people. Our pursuers were swifter than the eagles of the sky; they waited in ambush for us in the desert.[87]

We just kept marching forward without acknowledging their presence. We were wearing blinders because there was no benefit in acknowledging our demise. If there was a way to get out of this situation, we needed full concentration and determination. This seemed to irritate our pursuers as they began to make more noises and expose themselves longer and more frequently to us.

Then finally, they started to step out and stay visible, one by one. They fixed their gaze upon us and never wavered. With each being I passed, I could see their head turn and follow as I walked. Then, after I walked a bit further, they would start to follow behind me. I didn't pay them attention, but I could feel several footsteps walking within a couple lengths of me. It was as if they were a flock of buzzards, just waiting for us to show weakness before they consumed us. Eventually, some of the folks in the back would run up ahead and watch us walk by again. It seemed to be a pattern with them. Nobody spoke. The only noises heard were the increasingly excited footsteps and inaudible murmuring of our pursuers.

They became bolder with each step. One stood right in front of me some distance off and did not move. I walked around him, but he stood his ground, daring me to touch him. Then more appeared in front of Deputy Garza and me, so much so that we were unable to go around

---

[87] Lamentations 4:19

them. We eventually were forced to stop. We would have to confront them physically or just wait until they left because at this point they had formed a circle enclosing us.

They began to tighten the circle, closing in on us a bit at a time. There must have been about twenty-five of them, dirty, murmuring and moaning, as if they were starving dogs about to eat. Deputy Garza and I looked at each other. We were seeking answers in each other's faces, but finding none. Just like our initial escape, it had now boiled down to one action. We must fight and push through the mob or they would tear us apart. We knew what each other was thinking and knew it was the only way. It was now just a matter of timing to figure out when to fight and run.

Our backs were to each other as the animals closed in on us. Some licked their lips, others giggled, while some seemed enraged. They began pushing each other and jostling around as they came closer, as if they were competing for the first taste.

"We're going to have to take them off guard and become the aggressor," said Deputy Garza. I nodded. There was no other way.

Deputy Garza yelled and charged at the people and I followed, punching kicking and clawing our way through countless hands and bodies. Thud after thud I could feel the impact in my fists as I struck randomly at whatever form was in my vicinity. Amongst the blows from my hands were those for which I received. Often glancing, but numerous and quick, I began to take hit after hit. Some grabbed at me while others punched. Then I felt a crack on my legs while being slung to the ground. One of them had a big piece of wood and hit me square in the back of my legs. As I headed to the ground incapacitated, I knew I would be dead as soon as I was off my feet. Once I was on the ground, they'd take me apart and fight over the pieces.

I heard another crack and moan as I saw Deputy Garza go down as well. My shirt was being ripped, my hair pulled out as I fought desperately to keep from being overwhelmed. Eventually, the weight of the people and my exhaustion won out and I succumbed to my fate. Once they sensed my surrender, they began one by one to get off me and drag me on the ground to some unknown sacrificial location. I could hear Deputy Garza shouting at them while be dragged around as well.

Occasionally, a rock would hit my face as the bystanders were having fun with us again. Striking my face or stomach with a switch or rock, then falling back to giggle. They took us to a flat area and dropped our legs while keeping a foot on our neck. I saw one pull out a dull and rusty knife, while the rest delighted and giggled in anticipation. The one with the knife approached me, smiled and leaned down to look at my face. I was breathing manically, trying to shake lose and escape the subsequent torture. He stuck the tip of the blade just under my eye and yelps of joy erupted from the masses at the thought my eye being gauged. I began to scream in terror, wriggling desperately, and waiting for the moment of pain.

Suddenly, I felt the tension ease off my neck and could sense that our tormentors were moving back from us. I stood up quickly and saw a peculiar sight. It was difficult to comprehend given my state of terror and the massive amount of blood pumping through my body.

It was a man with a torch in rags. He was waiving it back and forth and the people were parting to let him through. It was as if they'd never seen fire before. They were swiping at him as he passed, but nobody touched him. In one hand he had the torch, in the other he held a chain pulling a cage similar to the one we had just escaped. This cage was metal and rusty, sitting on top of a four-wheel makeshift cart. The wheels squeaked as the man slowly pulled the cage along. He was doubled over a bit, looking as if the cage had the weight of the world behind it.

The man slowly reached us and stopped. One of the animals grabbed at the man's arm and he swung his torch at him and yelled, "Get" as one would do to a dog. The tormentor hissed and jumped back.

"These two are mine, go on and go back to where you came. They're going with me," the man commanded to the army of derelicts. They backed off, but did not go away. They watched him intently with an element of fear in their dark dead eyes.

The man looked over at us. Looked us up and down and sighed with sympathy.

"They hate the light, especially when you swing it at them. They're surprisingly easy to beat, once you know how. You guys don't look like you've got much left in you," the man said in a matter of fact manner. We didn't respond. I didn't know what to think about this person. He was simply dressed, like Huerta. He didn't have any particularly distinguishable features, like Huerta. His eyes were different though. Huerta's were dead, like his subjects. These were different. I couldn't put my finger exactly on what was different about these eyes, but they were. I didn't know whether this man was good or evil, but I did know that he temporarily saved our lives.

The man paused to give us a chance to engage with him, but neither of us were interested. He sighed again and said, "My name is Banez. If you want to be saved, get in the cage."

Chapter 12 – Banez.

The prospect of leaving one cage in order to get into another seemed farfetched for Deputy Garza and me. I couldn't imagine a more ridiculous thing to say to the two of us. However, I was frightened. I knew that horrible things would take place if we were to allow Huerta's people to get ahold of us. I also knew that I didn't want to be in a cage. I didn't know this Banez other than what the Ranger hold told me earlier, but that was just as tangible as the wind. How did we know that this guy wasn't partners with Huerta? Huerta's people seemed to know Banez and backed away from him rather quickly. Maybe he was their leader with Huerta. Maybe he makes deals with Huerta and they've been told to leave Banez alone. The difficult decision for us was to figure out if it was better to risk trying to escape alone or trusting someone with a cage whom we've never seen before and just after we escaped another cage. It was a perverse situation and it defied logic.

Banez seemed to have remarkable patience with us while simultaneously urging us along, "I've told you my name. I know all about Huerta. He knows who am as well. He doesn't like me. In fact, he hates me. I lead people from him. I save people from him. That's what I do. You may think that you've got choices here, but you don't. You can come with me or you will perish. That's it. And when I say perish...I mean perish in the most prolonged terrible way possible. Chains of darkness...a second death.[88][89]"

Deputy Garza shook his head and countered, "You almost had me until you added that poetic crap at the end. Everybody by the river is up to something. We were kidnapped and tortured. The Game Warden is probably dead or worse. I'm not getting in a cage because some

---

[88] 2Pet. 2:4.
[89] Rev. 20:14

nut job tells me so. You pushed these animals off of us, and we appreciate it, but we can bust

through their line right now and get out of here."

"Then where? You think they are going to just stop? You don't think they'll just come

get you later? They've got nothing better to do. This is their entertainment, maybe even food,"

said Banez. Deep down, I knew Banez was right. Like Deputy Garza, I didn't want to trade

being held hostage by one lunatic for being held hostage by someone else who might be just as

crazy. Then again, the prospect of fighting off these feral people seemed like an absolute

disaster…I was too tired to fight anymore. They were both gambles in a sense, although one

scenario seemed to be a sure loss, as far as I was concerned.

It came down to control, really. A lot of our critical decisions in life come down to how

much control are we willing to relinquish. The likelihood of being killed in a car accident has

always been far greater than the likelihood of being killed in an airplane crash. Yet, a far greater

population has a fear of flying than a fear of driving, which is a control issue. The thing is, the

mind of man plans one's way, but one's steps are directed by another.[90] I had a tendency to

follow my own plans, which means I would act in accordance to the stubbornness of my heart.[91]

My instinct was to avoid Banez and to go it with Deputy Garza against Huerta's people out in the

middle of nowhere. It would be a dumb decision, but it felt right because I would retain power

of my own actions until I was eaten alive by my enemies. Banez had proven that Huerta's

people feared him or at least gave him respect. If I went with Banez, I'd be caged and at his

mercy with no control over my situation, but I would likely survive long enough to give me

another chance to escape or come to find out that he was actually trying to help me. It should

have been an easy decision.

[90] Prov. 19:21
[91] Jer. 18:12

"The cage doesn't have a lock," Banez finally said, "I want to help you, but I'm sure not going to force you to do anything you don't want to do. Besides, I can't help you unless you want to be helped. What good would it do? The cage doesn't lock and there's only one of me. You can be confined to the bad or confined to the good.[92] It's too hot and dangerous for me to fight you on this, but you've got to make a decision soon. These guys can't keep to themselves forever."

I couldn't understand why both Huerta and Banez had cages that didn't lock. I was sure Deputy Garza caught this as well and had enough of these mind games. Deputy Garza shook his head and glared at me, imploring me to go with him. I looked at Banez and his dirty cage. I looked at the heavy chain tied to it and the cart underneath with its archaic wooden wheels. I wondered how such an average looking man could pull such a heavy and awkward load, with such a rough terrain, pulling an adult man or maybe two? I couldn't see how that was possible. Really, he was just pulling with one arm, he used the other to hold the torch. When he first appeared, Banez had that old chain slung over his shoulder. The pain must have been great to be lugging such a thing around. As the impossibility of Banez's task came to light, I began to question the matter. Maybe Deputy Garza was right. This guy might not be telling the truth. If so, then what happens? Is he going to take us to someone worse than Huerta? It seems impossible, but anything can be worse, relatively speaking.

Soon my decision was made for me as Deputy Garza gave me a quick glance and then punched the first man he saw, causing the crowd to back off ever so slightly. That opening was all he needed and he was off, disappearing in the darkness. Many ran after him, screeching and

---

[92] Rom. 6:18; 6:20

giggling into the night. The others turned their attention to us and began to creep ever so slightly closer and closer to us. Deputy Garza's timing had determined my fate.

I backed up further and further until my back was up against the cage. Deputy Garza was gone, I didn't want to go it alone and they were closing in on me. I looked over at Banez. I was giving my life over to him, so I tried to glean some kind of insight in his face. He didn't smile, nor did he push me to get inside…he just met my gaze. My eyes were fixed on his. He seemed patient for someone in such a situation, but it seemed as if this type of thing was pretty routine for him.

I crouched, got inside the cage and sat down. Banez shut the opening, turned around and slowly hauled me forward through the darkness. Huerta's people backed away as if there was a barrier around me. We were moving at half the pace of a walk, which was a fraction of the speed that Deputy Garza and I were originally moving. It didn't matter to me though because this cage felt like safety while Huerta's felt like a trap. For whatever reason, Banez's cage pushed Huerta's people away from me, but Huerta's cage drew them in to harass and torture.

I leaned my head against the bars, getting a bit of rest for the first time since I could remember. I let my muscles relax. Huerta's people continued to surround us and follow along. Every now and then one would get close and Banez would wave his torch at them and they'd scurry back in fear. I didn't bother to ask why or how this was possible, I didn't care…I just wanted to feel safe and comforted. I was weary and had carried heavy burdens, and I needed rest, which is what I was given.[93]

As we moved along, Huerta's people began to trickle off. It seemed like they were losing interest.

---

[93] Matt. 11:28

"The sun is coming up, they'll be headed back to Huerta soon. They don't like being out in the sun, most people don't here. We'll keep going though, until we get you to where you need to go," explained Banez as he handed me a little plastic water bottle through the cage.

I grabbed and drank it all down. I was so thirsty that I hadn't even thought of sharing. It was a small bottle and it might have been meant for both of us. I felt guilty, but it was the most satisfying drink I'd had in my life.

"It's yours. I'm fine. I brought it for you. I know you probably want more, but you've got to pace yourself, so you don't get sick and make things worse. I'll give you another in a little while," said Banez. He took the empty bottle and put it in his pocket.

It's difficult to imagine how important the basic things in life are until they're taken away. It's the delusion of the elite. I never assumed I was elite and on paper I probably wasn't, nor Game Warden Keller or Deputy Garza for that matter. Nobody was going to buy a product named after us, there were no pictures of us leaned up against luxury cars and there were no gates around our houses, but we were elite. If a person can wake up on any given morning without concern as to whether they were going to get food that day or be killed or have a place to stay, they would be part of the elite. If a person pondered *what to eat* and *not can he eat*, then that person is elite. Without contemplation, from the time I was born until the recent circumstances of my life, I was fed, clothed and more or less protected and sheltered. Throughout a normal day back in my old life, I would actually be disappointed to drink only water. I'd prefer something with flavor or carbonated or with caffeine or alcohol. I was disappointed to receive with absolutely no effort the most important life sustaining substance on the planet. Not just water, but clean, safe and pure water. That in of itself would be considered a miracle by a large percentage of the populous that share this world. Water that springs forth from a rock is a miracle by God, but cold clean water handed to you with no effort is routine.

This water that was given to me by Banez was the most precious gift I had ever received. It was a miracle. It was appreciated. I didn't care that it was limited and I didn't care that I needed to wait for more. I received it and was given a promise of more, which was a comfort I hadn't had in some time. It was not just a comfort, it was a luxury.

With that drink of water, I breathed and fell in and out of sleep until dawn's arrival. I didn't know how long I slept, but I felt the movement of the cage the entire time. The same steady pace, no rest, no relenting. I never heard Banez complain, groan or sigh. He just kept going. He pulled me all through the darkness and continued to pull me when the sun came up. I continued to slip in and out of consciousness only to be interrupted by Banez handing me a full water bottle, then retrieving the empty.

After the sun had been out for a while and a few more bottles of water, I moved around a bit in the cage. Banez noticed and handed me a piece of bread. I ate it and like the water, it was the best meal I ever had. It was thick, basic with little flavor and it was fantastic. My body needed every bit of nourishment held within that little piece of bread. Banez told me he'd give me more in a little while, but like the water, didn't want me to become ill.

The heat began to make its presence felt as the sun moved higher in the sky. It was starting to become unbearable. Banez put an old horse blanket over part of my cage to give me some shade.

"You can get out of the cage if you'd like. Huerta's people won't do anything right now," offered Banez. I didn't respond and I preferred the cage.

Banez marched on in silence with the same steady pace, no shade for himself and never stopping. As slow as we were going, he seemed to know the destination and the fact that we never stopped made me think we were making serious progress. I began to see a bit more greenery, which meant a bit more leaves on the scrub and a few weeks here and there. It was still an arid country.

Eventually, Banez broke his silence and spoke. He didn't look at me and he didn't stop pulling me, he just continued walking and looking forward and asked, "So, where are you going? I took you from Huerta's men, but you didn't say where you wanted to go."

It took a moment for me to grasp that this man was trying to have a conversation. I had been trying so hard to survive and living in such fear that this strange little question seemed foreign. He sounded like a cabdriver. I didn't understand how he could be so casual. "Well, I guess at the time I just needed to get away, but eventually I'd like to get back home," I replied.

"Where's home?"

"The States...can you get me there?"

"Yes, I take people to and from there all the time."

After Banez said this, a thought occurred to me. I wondered if he had anything to do with the kid that got burned. I couldn't remember his name. For the life of me I couldn't remember that kid. He was the sole reason I was into all this mess and for I couldn't remember that damn kid's name! What if he was sending me to my death as well? He had to have made arrangements with the cartel to burn the kid and all the others, right? If Huerta's bringing people back, then maybe Banez is taking people over!

I began to panic, but was able to force myself to gain some form of composure. Banez was doing all the work. He was basically dragging me home by himself. I could probably

169

escape once he got me to the river. I just needed to keep an eye on him and not let him know that I was on to him. Why else would he be doing this? Nobody is an altruist, especially down by the river. I just couldn't believe that such people existed.

"You know where I'm going, so tell me where you live," I inquired.

"I'm all over the place. Sometimes I'm in Mexico, sometimes I'm in the U.S. It just depends on where the need takes me," said Banez casually. This was as I suspected. He was another Huerta with no regard for the law or borders or anything really.

"So you move about like Huerta?" I asked. I was nervous about this question. I wanted to maintain a visage of naivety. I just couldn't help but feel like this man was some sort of rival to Huerta.

"No, I'm nothing like Huerta. Nobody gives me a cut of anything. Nobody pays me. I don't gain power. I don't command an army of evildoers. I go where I'm needed. That's all. Just like I did with you. I have the key...I open and no one will shut...I shut and no one opens[94], " Banez assured me.

"Then why are you doing this? What about those poor people that got burned? Huh? Did you lead them to be burned?" I had given it all away. I was no longer naïve.

Banez whirled around on me and for the first time, I saw an expression of anger. He dropped the chain to the ground and pointed his finger at me and said, "No! I don't lead people to be burned and never had! Do you understand me? You've taken the water and bread that I've given to you so you could be healed. I gave you bread, so that you may eat of it and not die.[95] You were thirsty and I gave water without payment.[96] Did Huerta give you water and bread?

---

[94] Rev. 3:7
[95] John 6:50
[96] Rev. 21:6

Did he? I saved you and dragged you through the night. I kept you safe. I'm taking you where you're supposed to go and you've given nothing to me and I haven't asked for anything. Have I? I do all these things for you and you accuse me of leading people to death? I don't lead people to death, I lead them to life. I don't take people across the river because they want to go. I take people to where they're supposed to go. I offered to take those people back home. I warned them of the dangers. I told them bad things would happen. They did not listen! Do you know what that's like? Do you know what it's like to know that some good people are headed for a horrible fate and there's nothing you can do about it? If they would have acknowledged me, I would have made their path straight.[97] I was a lamp to their feet and a light on their path I offered to help and they refused and they suffered mightily for it. They were burned alive and died for their rejection of me. That wasn't the first time either. It happens every day. Constantly I'm brushed aside while someone makes a deal with some coyote. They push me away and choose to bake to death in the back of a semi-truck somewhere. You can go. That cage is not locked. I told you that you could get out and walk, but you wanted me to drag you. You were comfortable being dragged. As soon as a moment of doubt hits though, you were ready to leave weren't you? Then what? Where are you going to go? What's your plan? I've been here longer than you've been alive. I know where to go and what to do, but…I'm not going to force you to do anything you don't want to do. I don't need to beg for you to allow me to help you."

I was silent and ashamed. I sat there in that cage with my head down, scared not of Banez, but of his rejection. The truth was that I didn't want to leave. I didn't want to be alone. I knew that I couldn't get home alone. I needed this man. I was certain that he would let go of

---

[97] Prov. 3:6

that chain and move on without me. In my despair, I felt something over my shoulder. I looked up and there was another water bottle. He gave me water. It was hot, I didn't know I needed water, but he knew I needed it and he gave it to me.

I felt the cage jolt and we began moving again. I looked up at Banez, that heavy chain over his shoulder pressing into his skin as he slowly pulled me along. He tilted his head back toward me again and gently aske, "So where are you going?"

I paused and finally said, "I'd like to go home. If you can get me home I'd like that. I can get out and help if you want. I'm tired of all this. I'm tired of strangers trying to kill me, I'm tired of being hungry, I'm tired of being thirsty and I'm tired. I want to go home."

"Then what?"

"I…I don't know what you mean. Home! I want to go home!" I sniped. I didn't want to play these games. Mr. Carlisle pulled this garbage on me a long time ago and he's the one that got me into this. My life would have never changed if I hadn't taken the assignment, if I hadn't decided to help that kid. What was that kid's name?

"I know you want to go home, but then what? Are you just going to go home and assume nothing has changed? Do you think your family is okay? Are you just going to close your eyes and wish everything back to normal?" Banez asked.

"I don't know."

"Do you know what normal is? Is normal the place you want to go?"

"I don't know. I want rest."

"I'm giving you rest. The weary and heavy burdened get rest from me.[98]"

"I don't want to deal with this anymore."

---

[98] Matt. 11:28

"It's been dealt and you have to deal with it."

I was tired and halfway insane by now. I did not want this conversation. If I wasn't wandering around somewhere near the Rio Grande I would have left this man by now. I fired back at him, "I tried to help a boy. That's all, and now my world is lost! That's not right! Don't you understand?"

"Yes…I do understand. I help people all the time. That's all I do and most reject me for it. Let me ask you something. Why did you want to help that boy?" asked Banez.

"I wanted to help him," I responded.

"Is that all? Weren't there some other reasons? Did you love him?" Banez asked skeptically.

"I don't understand the question," I responded.

"Did you love the person you were trying to help?"

"Sure."

"What's his name?" Banez asked casually. I knew he had me. He knew that I wasn't the type of person that just did good for the sake of doing good. I wanted points with the firm and I wanted myself to feel better about my pathetic life. That life I had was worthless. I wasn't bad, but I wasn't good. What are you if you're not bad or good? Are you a good person if you don't do anything bad? Are you a good person if you try and help someone for reasons other than just to help that person? If you leave no impact on anyone's life, are you a good person? At one time, I would have answered yes to all of these questions. Although motivated to a certain extent by self-interest, I came to the Rio Grande Valley to help a victim. Why would the motivation matter? In the end, my actions put my family in danger as well as myself. Who's to say if I would ever know the extent of my actions?

I did come to realize one important nuance. If I'd have been motivated by good, by truly wanting to help this kid and his companions, those people that were burned alive and then presumably killed…if I would have been motivated by good intentions…I would have ended this thing a long time ago. I would have looked in that briefcase, I would have questioned the motivation of others, and I would have turned the whole thing over to the authorities. I would not have been submissive to Mr. Carlisle. This man of whom I never knew whether he was a client, a partner or just a stranger. I would have asked the tough questions because I wanted to do right, not please the firm and further my career. Different motivations require different scrutiny. It's tough to say if the outcome would have been different, but I would have been good. I would have at least been good. Instead, I was nothing.

I was lost in thought for some time. Banez did not speak anymore, he just kept hauling me forward. Then, he stopped. Without saying a word, Banez dropped the chain to the earth and briskly walked off towards a patch of shrubs and knelt.

"What's going on?" I yelled to him, but he did not turn around. My heart fluttered a bit as I thought we might be in danger, but he wasn't moving. He was crouched low, looking at something.

I lifted the cage door. It squeaked with age and rust. I threw it open and crawled out stretching my stiff and pained body upwards to the sky. I quickly moved over to Banez to see what was on the ground.

It was a boot, Deputy Garza's boot. I recoiled a bit and my eyes darted around looking for Huerta's men.

"They're gone," Banez said roughly.

I could see the other boot about twenty feet away and bits and pieces of clothing scattered in different spots. I knelt next to Banez and he turned to me. His eyes watered. I was taken aback. He seemed to be holding back tears.

"I lost another one," he said to the ground. The man was downcast as if he were at a funeral.

"Maybe he made it," I suggested. Banez didn't reply. We both knew he didn't make it. Not without shoes and clothes. They got him and they tore him apart.

"I lost another one," Banez said again, "It's so simple. I offer a way out and you take it. It's so simple. You just get into the cage and I take you to freedom and safety. It doesn't matter which direction. The States or Mexico? It doesn't matter to me. I just want to save people. They don't want free help. It never makes sense. The people of Huerta, they think I own you when you get in the cage, that's how I keep them away. They respect the cage."

Banez shook his head, wiped his eyes and made it back to the cage and began to haul it forward again. I quickly caught up to him and he turned to me and said, "You need to learn to walk again. You stay out of the cage the rest of the way." I nodded in agreement.

We trudged on in silence as the surrounding terrain became a bit more lush and green. I could only assume that we were getting closer to the river. Signs of human life were cropping up here and there. An old plastic water bottle, a shoe or a can of something, just bits of litter popping up. Each piece of trash that I came across brought a piece of comfort with it. The more trash I saw, the closer we were to getting to civilization. I spent a good portion of my former life trying to hide or move trash. It was a constant cycle. Trash from the bathroom goes to the kitchen, which goes to the garage trash, which goes to the curb, which is picked up and taken to the landfill some miles away and hidden behind a ridge. Life was an infinite routine of gathering garbage, moving it to larger containers...the size was proportionate to proximity. The smaller

the receptacle, the closer the trash was to me. In my past life, garbage was a sign of incivility,

but after recent events, the correlation was flipped for me. I began to find comfort in the trash.

As my trust in the landscape grew, so did my trust in Banez. If this was a con, this was

the greatest and most pointless con I could remember. He shed a tear for Deputy Garza. This

man did not know Deputy Garza for all I know, yet he shed a tear for his fate. He'd given me

water, food and direction and had not asked anything in return. It could ultimately be a set up in

the end, but for what? I had no money and if he wanted to get rid of me for the cartel, he would

have done so by now without all of this effort. I knew logically that there likely was no harm

intended for me by this man. However, lingering doubts remained about such goodness for the

same reasons for doubts about evil. I wasn't worth it. If I wasn't worth the effort to harm, why

would I be worth the effort to help? What kind of person would put their life in danger, suffer

for dragging me through arid land and seek nothing. The good, the bad...none if it made sense.

Regardless, facts were facts. Banez was helping me, without condition. I was important

enough to be killed and to be saved. Huerta was obviously evil. Banez was good. He found me

in a desert land, and in the howling waste of a wilderness; he encircled me, cared for me,

guarded me as the pupil of his eye.[99] This goodness, this knowledge that someone was actually

trying to help me without expectations of something in return was something I had never really

experienced before. If someone in the past did want to help for the sake of being good, I would

not have recognized the intention or at least would have assumed an ulterior motive. This was

something new and energizing. Even though my body, mind and soul had been torn apart

throughout this ordeal, being taken care of and returning to the carefree life of an infant was a

---

[99] Deut. 32:10

relief. The buzz in my ear subsided. The pain in my stomach seemed to fade. The pressure in my skull was relieved. I felt as if I'd been cleansed.

We eventually crested a small upswing in the land and about a mile away I could make out the cluster of greenery drawn to the river. We had made it. I assumed that we'd be near Reynosa, but I didn't see anything remotely resembling a town. We were in the wild, but it felt more peaceful than any urban setting. It was hot, clear and the only movement was dirt and scrub in the wind. We walked on towards the river and I began to seek answers from Banez.

"Why do you help people? You don't know any of them. You don't know if I'm good or bad. What do you get out of it?" I asked.

Banez was thoughtful with his answer, "It's my duty to help. I don't get anything out of it other than I'm doing what I'm supposed to do. I don't get paid. I get by though. What does a man actually need in this life? As far as whether you're good or not....good or bad people don't matter much to me, I'm still going to help you. People still need to be saved."

"What about Huerta?" I asked.

"What about him?"

"Would you help Huerta?"

"He would never ask."

This was probably true. Huerta didn't seem like the type of person that would seek help from Banez. I understood Huerta about as much as I understood Banez.

"One thing I really don't understand about him," I asked, "why is he so open about whether we could leave? I mean…it was almost like he was bragging about his lack of security, that we could leave as we pleased. He told us that his people or the cartel's people would get us, but he never threatened to keep us. It's strange. That's not how I picture evil."

Banez walked in silence for a bit. It almost seemed like he was ignoring me, then he began to explain Huerta to me, "Huerta is clever and he's ahead of his time … or behind it. He knows that reality is far scarier than fables. He also knows that reality is what we make of it. It sounds like I'm contradicting myself, but it's true. I've seen my share of evil and power hungry people. I've seen normal people do crazy things out of fear and anger. In the past, controlling information was a form of power, but now I'm not so sure. I think Huerta invites people to know what's out there because it's scarier to a lot of people than staying with him. Think about your old life back at home. You turn on the television or computer or look at your phone and all you see is constant death and destruction. It's evil out there. People want somebody scary to be around to protect them from the other scary people. If you're the type of person who's brave enough to go out into the desert and risk being killed by bandits or criminals, then Huerta probably doesn't want you. He needs folks who he can control. He wants the weak and scared. There's more and more of those nowadays…the weak and scared. People are barraged by outrage, anger and violence. They want a leader…any leader, good or bad. Someone to keep them safe."

He was right. I noticed that in my life as well. Back home, the more free time I had, the more I paid attention to the news and the anger. A person doesn't need to watch more than thirty minutes of news a day. These news shows don't add any new information beyond that thirty minutes. All they accomplish is repetition. Over and over I was told that the world was awful, until such thoughts and visions became a reflex… triggered without thought or cause. Everything was scary. Everything was scary and everyone was trying to get each other until a person snapped! Yet, most people really weren't out to get each other. Most folks weren't special enough to have a conspiracy against them. So then people would just sit, waiting for the terror that never came. They waited and waited for the impending doom they were told was coming, clenching their teeth and grinding them in fear and anger. A person could just gone for a walk to clear their minds, but they don't. One could build something, but they refuse. A person could help a neighbor, but they hate their neighbor! They sit and wait and rage. They don't know how to solve the world's problems, but they want them solved. We all want the fear to go away and we want to be safe…at any cost. The Fuhrer Principle.

However, to suffer is to liberate. All of the worldly things that frightened and angered me so much were gone. Poof! I no longer cared when a politician lied or which group was being marginalized or how outraged I should be about every single hot-button issue forced into my brain. That was gone. All I cared about was not dying. All I cared about was returning to what may or may not be left of my family and former life. I didn't want to be tortured or kidnapped. I wanted to stop the bad guys from doing more harm. I wanted to escape. Every person that showed up on my computer or television screen to shout me into a state of fear in order to sell more advertisement space were all muted and removed from my subconscious. They were dead and I was born anew.

I was beaten, starved, kidnapped, lost and abandoned in a desert only to be rescued by perspective and the realization that while bad and not-so-good people surrounded us, there were truly good people among them that were far more powerful than the all the others. Huerta and his followers didn't touch Banez. For whatever reason, his light shined bright enough to ward off the dark.

"We are close to our departure," announced Banez.

"Why? I thought you can come and go across the river as you please," I was worried that he would leave me.

"I can do whatever I want, but just because I can doesn't mean that I will. You decide how you're going to get across. A few miles downstream is the official crossover. If you don't want to cross there, then cross up ahead there and someone I'm sure will pick you up. It'll be up to you to make sure they know you're not a threat," instructed Banez. I nodded and we walked silently a little bit more until he started in on more grandiose instructions.

"When you get back there, you're going to see the world differently. This will be permanent. Nothing is going to fit into the neat categories that they want. Nobody wants to deal with outliers. You are either on one side of the line or the other, but that's not how it is. You've got to see it all from above, in three dimensions, not on the ground. You understand? Don't let anyone deceive you in any way, because the day will not come until the rebellion occurs and the man of lawlessness is revealed, the man doomed to destruction.[100] He will oppose and will exalt himself over everything that is good, so that he sets himself up in a place of good, proclaiming himself to be good.[101] The secret power of lawlessness is already at work; but the one who now holds it back will continue to do so till he is taken out of the way.[102] Then the lawless one will be revealed, and will be overthrown with the breath of mouth and destroyed by the splendor of the coming good.[103] The coming of the lawless one will be in accordance with how evil works. He will use all sorts of displays of power through signs and wonders that serve his lies, and all the ways that wickedness deceives those who are perishing. They perish because they refused to love the truth and so be purified.[104] Because they refuse to love truth, a powerful delusion will be sent so that they will believe the lies and so that all will be condemned who have not believed the truth but have delighted in wickedness.[105] But you need to always to be thankful for the good

---

[100] 2 Thes. 2:3
[101] 2 Thes. 2:4
[102] 2 Thes. 2:7
[103] 2 Thes. 2:8
[104] 2 Thes. 2:9-10

people, because they are first fruits to be saved through the sanctifying work of good and through belief in the truth.[106] You are being asked to share this glory.[107] Do you understand Martin? Do you know that your life is now forever different and your purpose is not to keep track of others' achievements and your own accomplishments or worldly things? You are now part of a bigger machine. Nobody wants to be a part of a bigger machine than them, but that is misguided arrogance. You have a purpose and your purpose is to fit with all the other good peoples' purposes in order to make the world good. You must outnumber the Huertas and the Carlisles," Banez finished with eyes ablaze, staring deep within me.

"Carlisle?" I asked.

"I know him as well as Huerta," Banez replied.

Banez led me a hundred yards away from the river, put his hand on my shoulder and looked me in the eyes. He smiled with approval, handed me some water and bread and bid farewell. I watched him walk away until he disappeared behind some scrub, never to reappear.

I sighed, turned and made my way to the river.

---

[105] 2 Thes. 2:11-12
[106] 2 Thes. 2:13
[107] 2 Thes. 2:14

Chapter 13 – The Return.

It was a messy return. Because I trudged across the Rio Grande instead of going through the checkpoint, I would understandably be looked upon with great suspicion. I wasn't sure how many Anglos crossed the border back into Texas illegally, but I guessed most of them that did so were not morally sound. Other than an old fashioned kidnapping, why would someone do such a thing?

Regardless, I was willing to risk dealing with the river more so than dealing with the Mexican border guard when I had no identification, smelled and looked like I'd slept in the bottom of an outhouse. Those guys wouldn't have let me just pass without asking a couple of questions and checking to make sure their unofficial employers weren't looking for me. Finding a scared, dirty American wearing the remains of a business suit without a wallet was like finding some rich old lady's Shih Tzu that wandered off. It could mean a little extra money for someone at the very least.

Even if I would have been able to get past the Mexican border guards, there was always the chance that one or two American guards were on the same payroll as the Mexican guards. If that was the case, I'd have been in real trouble. The American patroller wasn't going to bother sending me back over, he would just separate my head from my body and roll me into the river and collect his payment.

No, I was going to take my chances that some rancher would hopefully shoot above my head for a bit and then come over and investigate. I would trust that rancher any day over a government official. That rancher was on nobody's payroll and didn't want to be on anybody's payroll but his own. That rancher did what he did in life because he didn't want to be beholden to anyone. Those ranchers could be Latino, Anglo or anything for that matter and they all had the same fanatical desire for freedom pumping through their veins. Those Tejanos…some of those families got those ranches from the King of Spain, before Texas was Mexican, Texan or American. If that family was lucky enough to fight off the Anglos trying to steal their land back in the eighteen hundreds, they sure as hell weren't going to give it up to anyone else.

To be clear, none of those ranchers wanted anyone walking around their property either. The good news was that instead of arresting me or detaining me, they would just shoot at me and if I didn't run, they would either shoot until they hit me or come up and ask what the heck I was doing on their land. They may even feed me if they believed me or…they may just put a hole in me. It all depended on how they woke up that morning and who was pissing them off more, the immigrants or the federal government.

My mindset was to stumble upon a ranch and hopefully be confronted by a rancher or one of his ranch hands. That would involve less walking. I would either be shot or helped, either way I wouldn't need to walk anymore. Without Banez handing me water and dragging me around, I was almost helpless. I barely knew the man, but I sure did miss him. He seemed to be the only one I had come across whose actions were pure. On the selfish side, he gave me water and carried me.

If I somehow got past the ranch without coming into contact with anybody, then I'd have to walk far into the scrub without food or water. If I kept going without succumbing to the elements or dehydration, I'd need to walk until I got to civilization or a check point on a highway. The highway check point would be not much different than the border check other than it was geographically less removed from the cartel, but who's to say for sure?

I walked amongst the scrub until I came across some barbwire, which was a welcomed sight. It meant that I was close to that sweet semi civilized unwelcoming institution of a ranch.

The barbwire was the first sign of life…the first hope of having that suspicious twelve gauge pointed right at my face. Someone had pushed the barbwire down to the ground, there was a shirt wrapped around it and a couple of plastic water bottles, which were either the last drink before freedom or capture depending on the luck of the crosser. The bottles looked new, so the travelers must have been to that spot fairly recently. Not far down the fence line was a tree with a purple stripe painted on it. It looked relatively fresh. The purple meant no trespassing, any Texas hunter could tell you that. It also meant that the rancher hadn't had time to mend the fence, which means he'd be back. If the rancher carried purple paint with him, then he was diligent and would come back to fix that fence I assumed. It also meant that he might put a hole in me, especially if he's chasing other border crossers ahead of me.

I decided that there would be no sneaking around. I wanted the ranch owner to see me a mile away. More importantly, if it was a hunting lease and if it was hunting season, I didn't want to be game for a bad shot sportsman.

I trounced about in as open a territory available, avoiding the scrub and intermittent trees as much as possible. I wanted the person watching the land to see me before I saw them.

Sure enough, it wasn't long before I heard a loud pop in the distance. I stopped for a second, just to make sure I didn't have any new holes in my body and then looked around. I felt comfortable that whoever fired the shot would have killed me if they wished, but that comfort was fleeting as I was still out in the middle of nowhere and shots had been fired. I saw a figure in the distance, standing next to an all-terrain vehicle with cowboy hat and presumably boots…gun pointed in the air. We both stood still and waited, staring at each other from far enough away that we couldn't make out each other's faces. I didn't need to see his face. I could see by the way he was standing what he was all about. Down here, body language is important.

Distance between folks is a norm and people need to form a perception of each other based on shape, not facial expression. A person needs to know who they are because if you don't know yourself, nobody else will and it's suspicious. Nobody gets to ask the ubiquitous, "who am I?" question down here. It's too much of a luxury.

After a significant pause, he fired off two quick ones, above my head to make sure there was no confusion. I calmly raised one hand and began to make the hike towards him…straight line, not fast, no meandering either. He laid the gun across his arms and leaned up against the ATV and waited as I walked. He wasn't going to make an effort to help me just yet, but he didn't seem like he was going to kill me either…just yet.

I got about ten yards away and he squared the gun on me, so I stopped and raised my hands. "That's good enough right there," the rancher shouted. I sucked in shallow breathes, afraid that I would spook him with noisy breathing. We both stood statuesque, neither willing to break the silence.

The rancher cleared his throat, sighed a bit and said, "So…what's the story? What the hell are you doing on my property? It looks like you've been rolling around in the mud with that little suit of yours. Don't make much sense now, does it? Was it cocaine or something else somebody gave you?"

"Long story," I replied.

"We're not going anywhere, so let's have it," he eased the gun barrel down slightly pointing it in my direction as he replied. The rancher still held the gun casually, confident he could use it on me before I could get to him I assumed.

I left out a significant amount of details when recalling my story to the rancher. I more or less told him I was down here for business for a big law firm, got kidnapped and escaped. He nodded and didn't bother asking any follow-up questions for that matter. This sort of thing must be more common than I assumed.

"They put you in a stash house?" he asked. I nodded. "Yep, that's what they do. Especially with guys like you, all suited up and what not," he concluded, shaking his head a bit.

The rancher waived me to come closer and I obliged. This felt like I'd earned some trust and sympathy, although he stuck the barrel of the gun in my back and proceeded to frisk me. Seemed reasonable to me.

I hopped on the ATV with him and he drove us to a house, making me sit on the porch while he went inside. I could see him pull out his phone and a rush of panic took me again. I knew this would happen, but now that I was somewhat safe, I didn't want the authorities getting involved. Not now…not being so close to getting out of this.

I made an ill-advised decision and entered his house while he was on the phone. As soon as our eyes met, I knew that I hadn't thought the whole thing through. Within a matter of seconds, the butt of the rancher's gun was violently colliding with the bridge of my nose. I heard a loud crack and then things faded out as I hit the floor.

I don't know how long I was out, but I woke up in a police car. I wasn't in the safe house of a rancher. I wasn't with Banez. I wasn't home. It was over.

The pain in my nose hit me along with the pain that things were now out of my hands. Fear, pain and oddly relief were racing through my throbbing head. I felt the warm flow of blood pushing through the tissues jammed up my nostrils. The rancher must have broken my nose. My head hurt, my nose hurt and I was at the point of reckoning.

I was either going to be helped or killed and there was nothing I could do about it. I sat up and looked around the car, trying to get the fuzz out of my brain. I was able to focus on the

186

front seats, which was miraculous given my mental state. There was only one officer in the car and he was Anglo. For some reason that gave me relief. It didn't make any sense really, I mean I've been helped and attacked by folks of Latino heritage, so why I'd all of a sudden be safe with a white officer over a Latino officer didn't really make any sense. I mean, Mr. Carlisle was white and he put me into the whole mess. Such thinking goes back to the time of cavemen. A person felt safe around familiarity. It was animalistic. Logic didn't play into it. Maybe I thought a white person would be less accepting of the corruption, like it was an anomaly and not a way of life, but I should have known better. Most folks have a price. Maybe Anglos were just more apt to dance around the subject and feign being appalled by grift. It didn't really matter down in the valley. Anybody could work for anybody. You had to serve somebody. You could be a slave to evil or a slave to righteousness, but you had to be a slave.[108] There was no middle ground.

The officer's eyes met mine and he cheerfully greeted me, "Good morning sunshine." His voice sounded like chain-smoking gravel. He looked to be in his fifties and so out of shape that he couldn't chase down a criminal if the existence of the world depended on it.

"Old Troy says he found you wandering around on his property. Says you weren't a problem until you tried to pay him a visit inside his house. That was dumb, boy. Don't you know not to come inside another man's house without permission? Your lucky he didn't kill you. That must mean he believes your story," he said, glancing in the mirror. He gave me a wink that sickened me.

I didn't say anything. I was still trying to get my bearings.

---

[108] Rom. 6:15-18

"They take you to a stash house?" the officer asked. I nodded. "Was it one of those shacks down there?"

I shook my head and answered, "No…I think it was underground." The air left the car. As soon as I said that the stash house was underground everything changed. The officer's cheery eyes immediately dropped all emotion and he went silent. The air seemed stale all of a sudden and I could feel an immediate tension. He was quiet. Now he glanced at me in the mirror with cold eyes that seemed to have turned black. It was the steely look someone gives when things turn serious and dangerous.

We approached a stoplight and the officer pulled a U-turn. He didn't warn me and he turned the car quickly enough for me to feel the tires pulling on the road. I began to panic. This was it. Where was he taking me? I should have kept things vague about Hureta's underground lair.

"Excuse me…where are we going?" I asked feigning naivety.

"We got to get you checked out and make sure there's nothing physically wrong with you. I was in such a hurry to get you to the station, I forgot to take to the hospital first. Just a precaution," assured the officer. I frantically looked around, trying to get some clues as to who this guy was and where we were going.

"I'm Martin, what should I call you, officer?" I asked, just throwing stuff at the wall by this point.

"Well, you don't need to call me officer for starters. I'm with the sheriff's department. Senior Deputy Bauer. Just call me Deputy Bauer. Better yet, why don't you just stay quiet for a while? You're probably suffering from a concussion," Deputy Bauer responded. I knew that name. I knew it! I just couldn't remember where. It was bad, I knew it was bad.

"I'm just glad I'm finally safe. When can I get back home?" I asked frantically trying to remember why I recognized his name.

"Soon enough. Your health and safety are my number one priority… you can count on that. Nobody's getting to you…they'd have to go through me," said Deputy Bauer.

"Where's your partner?"

"Don't need one. Where's yours?"

He looked back at me in the mirror again, irritated that I was talking. I kept quiet. I noticed that the landscape was not becoming any more urban from when we began the drive. If he was taking me to the hospital, why did it seem like we were going further into the backcountry? There was little doubt now…I was going to die.

My heart beat rapidly, with the sounds of the outside world being drown out by the rushing blood in my ears. The Deputy would occasionally look at me, probing my face for some sort of tell. Despite my internal panic, I gave him nothing to look at or to think about. I carefully reached for the door handle, only to find nothing. It was a sheriff's car. Could I kick the window out? No, I was positive that had been attempted in this past.

I sat staring at the scrub quickly passing by my face, desperately trying to come up with a plan. I'd come so far, survived so much, only to be taken back to my captors or just flat out murdered…and my family. What's this guy going to do to my family? I remembered them…their faces or the ideal of them? Did I care about them or losing what they represent? Was I scared that I'd have to start over in a life lessor than now? Was I sad?

I wasn't sad… I was trying to survive. A person doesn't get sad unless there is time to be sad. I had no time. I was not thinking enough to be sad or scared. This was reptilian. This was the lowest part of my brain. Stressed from extreme elements, not ideals or disappointment. It was my life being simplified in its purist form. I would either survive or not. That was it. There was nothing more to it. This man, this officer of the law, the law of survival… at that moment in time, represented life or death. That was all that mattered. Worrying about my family was pointless if I was going to die. I couldn't worry. I didn't have the ability to worry. I was thinking from one beat to the next. Strike or flee. Hide or seek. This was the simplest and most rapid form of thinking fueled only by the chemical energy from a dose of homegrown adrenaline…a renewable resource.

I couldn't wait for this deputy to dispose of me. I had no plan, but didn't need one because if I were to get out of this situation it would be by chance or a mistake. I saw the Deputy make a call, which was brief, more or less a grunt confirming something. He never made a radio call about me. He was confirming with someone that he had me, but not through official means. This meant that he was expected to be somewhere and I was gong to delay it. The harder I made it for him to take me the better chance I had of survival. I just needed to become an anchor for a while.

I saw a truck pulled over far off in the distance.

"I need to use the restroom," I said.

"Come again?" responded Deputy Bauer.

"It's coming out…I need to use the restroom. I…I was too scared before. I just didn't know I had to go. I need to go now!" I demanded.

"Nope," the Deputy responded.

"Seriously? You're just taking me to the hospital, I don't understand why I can't use the restroom before I get treatment," I argued.

"I don't have time for this. We're not stopping," the Deputy insisted.

190

"It's going to come out one way or the other."

He looked at me hard, probably assuming I hadn't come up with an escape plot yet and likely not wanting to draw suspicion to what he was doing, he wanted to appease me as long as he could. Even sharks roll back their eyes before they bite. It's always better to take out a victim peacefully. Let them bleed out.

Deputy Bauer pulled over about fifty yards before the old truck that I spotted on the side of the road. Somebody was messing around under the hood and waived at us when we stopped. I assumed he was hoping we were there to help him out, which was ironic given what fate had in store for this poor stranded man.

Deputy Bauer paid the man no notice. He was on a schedule. He slammed his door shut and came around to the back and opened my door. I immediately kicked him down and fell on top of him. He was cursing me and was trying to pull himself up. I just kicked and kicked at whatever I could make contact with. Whatever would delay things and cause attention is what I had to do. I screamed, yelled and kicked. My face felt as if it would burst from the blood straining to get out. Beat after beat, I kicked and yelled, hoping to catch an eye or a nose with my heel.

I heard the stranded motorist yell something at us...trying to find out if the Deputy needed help. Dust engulfed us as I continued to strike Deputy Bauer...yelling that he was kidnapping me all the while. Blood, dust and sweat were all that I could sense, until I felt a blow to my head. I stopped and staggered, looking down at those old boots of the Deputy, now standing over me and pushing me back into the car.

I tried to yell again, but it was just a gurgled murmur as I lost my bearings. I was on my back in the seat, trying to raise my head enough to see through the dust, but I saw nothing.

I heard the man ask if everything was okay to Deputy Bauer and then I heard a shot, then silence. With a thump, the man's body was thrown on top of me, face to face, eyes still open while his blood dripped all over me. The door slammed, car started and I could feel the tires slip as the Deputy hit the gas. He cursed and muttered under his breath as we left.

We drove for some time, all the while with the corpse staring at me. He shook as we bounced over potholes and bumps. Every time the corpse bounced, more of his blood would drip from his mouth onto me. I had to turn my head to keep the blood from running into my eyes and mouth. I didn't want to taste the dead man's blood.

The car came to an abrupt stop, forcing the corpse and me to roll off the back seat onto the floorboards. Now I was on top of the body, doing everything in my will to keep our faces from touching. I'm not sure why this bothered me so much given the amount of atrocities I had seen so far. Why at that moment in time was I so fearful of touching this mass? It must have been some ancient genetic code of repulsion for the dead. If you touch a corpse, you'll be unclean for seven days or you must not enter a place where there is a dead body or you'll be unclean.[109] [110] I'm not sure if people even thought of such things anymore. Maybe it was just creepy. Regardless, I did not want to touch a dead body.

The back door flung open and I was dragged out onto a dirt road, my face hitting the ground. My eye could neither open nor shut due to the coagulation of my blood, the blood of a dead man, dust and sweat all combined to make a paste sealing me shut. I struggled to roll to my side, still handcuffed, in order to see the fate that was bestowed upon me. My cheek to the ground, vision still blurred, I saw two little shiny black shoes emerge from a black town car across the dirt road. It must have been waiting on us. I heard chuckles and mutterings, some

---

[109] Num. 19:11
[110] Lev. 21:11

stern talks between Deputy Bauer and the black shoes. I even heard mention of Huerta, followed by some low and somber mumbles.

Eventually I heard the owner of black shoes chuckle arrogantly and Mr. Carlisle's presence was confirmed. I knew those little shiny shoes belonged to him. I also knew things were now hopeless. Mr. Carlisle will make my bad situation worse. He was purchasing me or claiming me, the specifics of the arrangement between him and the Deputy were not clear, but there was some sort of arrangement. Mr. Carlisle had his hands in everything. I knew I'd be his.

They approached and I became privy to their conversation. "Well deputy, you pulled a number didn't you? Cold blooded...that's why I like you. Just killed a guy for the hell of it! Very nice. I'm not much of a murderer myself. I like to actually have a goal in mind when I do things. From the looks of it, you seem to enjoy this type of thing?" stated Mr. Carlisle to Deputy Bauer.

I could hear the anger in Deputy Bauer's voice when he responded and I knew that anger myself, "Nope! I had to. I don't enjoy killing and I don't enjoy you!"

"But you keep calling me, don't you?"

"I had to, that's part of the deal."

"That's right fat man. I'm always part of the deal. Well, your bloodlust is your own business. I find that I like dealing with bad guys like yourself better than the good ones. I can trust the bad ones...you're predictable. I know you'll make a logical decision and that you'll do anything with the right leverage. These good ones, you never know when they want to be a martyr," said Mr. Carlisle.

The Deputy ignored Mr. Carlisle's pokes and seemed to be in a hurry to get the act over with, "Here he is, take him and be done with it."

193

"Sure, but I'm not messing with the other one. If you would have kept him alive, I might have given you something for your troubles. I've got some associates that could have made some money off of him. But…you killed him, so it's just a matter of digging a hole and I don't dig holes," said Mr. Carlisle.

"Yeah, I reckon you haven't done much with your hands," retorted the Deputy gruffly.

"Well, idle hands are the devil's workshop[111], so…we'll call it even," said Mr. Carlisle.

The Deputy ignored him and began to drag me towards Mr. Carlisle's car. I was limp and didn't have the energy to fight. The only thing that could save me was some intervening action because I was no longer capable of anything. This was the opposite of the American dream. My whole life I read and heard about rugged individualism. Pulling ourselves up by our own bootstraps. Solving problems ourselves. A man could lose his entire family through divorce, be miserable, never see his kids, miss funerals, anniversaries, church, charities, health, but as long as he's got a story of building himself up to be a success, he can take a picture in front of a fancy car and people will praise him. He can ruin lives, put others at risk and work himself to death, but if he's a self-made man he deserves our respect. If he's really living the American dream, he might even give a little back to those in need. He might make a foundation, named after himself of course, and after he's done paying all the employees of this foundation, after he's used the money of this foundation to pay some bills, hold some taxable income, sponsor some golf tournaments, then a bit will go to help build a shelter for lost cats or dogs or something and it will be good because that's what good people do. A person can do anything, as long as they work hard and have the will to disregard any other aspect of their life. A person has to have the look that deputy gave me in the mirror…that look that says that all other things in life

---

[111] Prov. 16:27

are disregarded. Morals, ethics, right and wrong…dead! That's the secret…working hard and willing something to success. It would be easy, yet only a small percent of the population seems able to achieve this very simple act. A man who mowed the lawns in my neighborhood worked harder and longer than any person I had ever known, but I had yet to see a picture of him in front of a car or a private plane. He followed the formula, work hard, will power and so forth, yet he was not rich. He must have not wanted it bad enough, because that was all one needed to do. A person just needs to want something bad enough and then it becomes theirs…or so we are told.

I had a head wound, was handcuffed by a law enforcement officer, was exhausted and malnourished and I wanted to escape. Oddly enough, I could not will the handcuffs off of my hands. I could not remove the gun from the Deputy and win my freedom. I was not living the American dream. I was not a rugged individualist. I was broken and the only thing I could possibly do at that moment was wait and assume something would happen to save me. I could only accept the fact that I needed to be saved. That was the only individual act I could muster. Only by grace could I be saved.[112] I accepted that fact.

So, I was dragged across the road by an overweight middle-aged corrupt deputy to someone whom I could only presume was some sort of manifestation of Satan himself. I waited…I waited to be saved…saved by anything that may come along.

The Deputy dropped my legs as soon as I was a few feet away from Mr. Carlisle's car. I turned my head to look down the dirt road, my cheek rubbing in the grit. I stared into the distance, seeing the heat waves in the air, noticing for the first time how the air was excessively hot. I saw a speck on the horizon, with a bit of dust coming up with it. It was a car. A car was coming towards us. That was the intervening factor that I needed.

---

[112] Eph. 2:8

From my spot on the ground I could see both Mr. Carlisle and Deputy Bauer turn towards the oncoming car. Deputy Bauer squinted his eyes for a bit and said, "It's a ranger." He put his hand on his hip, almost in a relaxed manner as if to indicate that he's glad that he might be caught. He had a dead body in his car and me on the ground, so I couldn't imagine the story he'd come up with to get out of this.

Before I could finish my thought, my ears rang with a loud pop! The Deputy flew back next to me onto the ground, eyes wide and staring at me in terror. He reached towards me, gurgling through the blood quickly choking off his air supply. Then he stopped and his eyes grew dark and still. Dead eyes staring at me again.

"Well, one of us shot a deputy. I guess every now and then, I've got to do a little dirty work for myself," announced Mr. Carlisle.

I couldn't speak just yet. I was in disbelief although nothing should have surprised me by then.

"What am I going to do about this ranger? Is he going to believe you shot deputy beer belly? Not likely. The good thing is that we've got two bodies and you in handcuffs. Seems just confusing enough to take advantage of the situation, don't you think? Sometimes chaos is the best ally in scenarios like these. People always talk about chess versus checkers, like it's so prestigious to know how to play chess! It's a game! It doesn't matter if you're playing chess, checkers or candy land because I'm going to grab that damn game and knock the pieces across the room!" exclaimed Mr. Carlisle.

He seemed to be getting amped up as the car approached, like he was excited about the whole prospect of a confrontation.

The car pulled up and it was the Ranger from the restaurant, Ranger J.C. Torres. He stepped out of the car and a look of astonishment came over his face. He spotted the Deputy and rushed over immediately. The Ranger bent down and put his ear to the Deputy's chest and put his finger to his neck. I saw Mr. Carlisle behind him, franticly fumbling in his pocket. Dread flooded me when I realized what was happening.

"No!" I exhaled.

The Ranger stood up and whirled around just as the pop of Mr. Carlisle's gun went off. Ranger Torres hit the ground and groaned. I began to shake, knowing I had lost my chance to escape.

Mr. Carlisle stood for a moment, looked at me and said, "Two in a day...that's more than I do in a year most of the time. I hate getting too dirty. Son, I'm not sure why this hasn't sunk into you yet, but no matter what anybody tells you, bad guys are usually the winners. It's a matter of who's worse and who can control their circumstances best. You grew up thinking it's good guys versus bad guys. That's silly. It's always been bad guy versus bad guy...good guys are too cowardly to fight! The Deputy I killed, he stopped more crimes and saved more lives than you ever will in your entire life! And he was a piece of garbage. He would have killed you just to get a one percent raise at the end of the year. He'd have planted cocaine on you if it meant filling a quota by the end of the month. So who did more good works in their short little lives, you or that fat, corrupt, greedy deputy? I'll tell you who..."

Bam! Mr. Carlisle fell back against his car! He put his hand on his stomach, trying to comprehend that he was actually shot. People have probably wanted to shoot Mr. Carlisle, but few probably were willing to pull the trigger as he always seemed to be once removed from blame. He looked up in shock at the Ranger still on the ground, "Son of a...?" Before Mr.

197

Carlisle bothered to finish his sentence he had jumped in his car and whoever was driving sped the car away kicking up dust all over the Ranger and me.

I rolled to my side to see the Ranger putting a makeshift tourniquet on his leg. He looked at me and said, "Just the leg. I'll be alright if I can get us back without bleeding out. Don't want to call the sheriff's department out here. I'll get us to the hospital and get some folks I trust to watch out for us there. Hurts like hell though."

We both sat there, dumbfounded and breathing hard for a bit before the Ranger finally dragged himself up and limped over to the Deputy. He grabbed the keys, to the handcuffs off of me and motioned for me to get in the backseat, which I obliged. Ranger Torres exhaled and hobbled into the front seat, started up the car and did a quick turnaround to head to town. We drove for a minute until I realized Mr. Carlisle got away. I began to panic.

"What about Mr. Carlisle?" I gasped.

"Who?" asked Ranger Torres.

"Mr. Carlisle! He was right there! He...he was behind the whole thing and he's getting away! You've got to stop him," I pleaded.

"Carlisle?"

"The guy who was just there talking!"

"Ah, hell son. That name's just as meaningless as the rest of them. They all have aliases."

"But he's always been there...from the beginning. He got me into all this...he's behind it!"

"I'm not in the judging business. I'm in the protection business. I'm trying to save you. I'll catch the bad guys, but I got to save you first. You understand? I can't just lock up a guy cause you say he's bad. That's not my job," explained Ranger Torres with some extraordinary patience for someone who was shot in the leg.

"But Huerta…he and Carlisle were probably working together…don't you see?" I was getting delirious at this point.

"Yes, son! I see. Huerta, Carlisle, Bauer, Hitler, Bin Laden and so on…I see it all son. You've seen a lot and believe me, I've seen a lot. I've seen all of them. Sometimes they sneak up on you, sometimes they come shooting at you. I've seen them all and I know them all. It doesn't matter, it's the same beast. It's got teeth and wings and breathes fire. Everyone's running around like ants, but you've got to lock up the beast. He's roaming and it's not my job to lock him up. I just get rid of as many ants I can catch and keep you from getting bit or at least help you after you've been bit. The evil…that's out of my pay grade. Every damn cop show I've ever seen shows those poor saps drinking in some dive bar, complaining that they can't stop the bad guys because they just keep coming and coming, that it's all pointless, blah, blah, blah. That's not realty. Evil was there before I became a ranger and evil will be there after I stop being a ranger. My job's not to cure the world of evil. What kind of job is out there that requires you to cure the world of evil? We're not gods. Nope, my job is to try my damnedest to protect the rest of us, hopefully prevent others from falling in with the bad guys and most importantly…make sure I don't forget that I can't stop it all on my own. When I was a child, I spoke and thought and reasoned as a child. Now I see things imperfectly, like puzzling reflections in a mirror, but one day I'll see everything with clarity[113]. You ever hear that before son?"

---

[113] 1 Cor. 11-12

We sat quietly for a moment and the Ranger looking at me then down at his leg, then back at me with a quizzical look. Ranger Torres finally sighed and shouted, "Damn it Martin! I took a bullet for you! Give me a damn break!"

So, I did.

CPSIA information can be obtained
at www.ICGtesting.com
Printed in the USA
BVHW030212240619
551791BV00001B/80/P